Dawn Knight
BOOK ONE

Andre LaVelle

DEDICATION

To my loving, beautifully imperfect family —
Even when I struggle to show it, I love you with all my heart, and there isn't a day this journey hasn't put you in my thoughts and my prayers. The distance this path created between us has never changed how deeply I care.
Every step I've taken in my creative grind has been with you in mind: to build something lasting, a legacy that will help and inspire us and our children to dream bigger, move fearlessly, and walk fully in the potential our ancestors fought so hard to give us.

CONTENTS

ACKNOWLEDGMENTS

First, to my mom – thank you for always, *always* encouraging my creativity and still pushing me to dream bigger. You've been my first cheerleader and my forever "you got this."

To my family and friends who ride for me and support every wild entrepreneurial move I make – thank you for pushing me, hyping me, and holding me down.

To that thing inside me that just won't let me quit, even when walking away feels like the easiest option – you're the reason this book exists.

To everybody who's ever said a kind word, made a purchase, shared a post, or just sent good vibes when the negativity sat heavy on my shoulders – I feel that love, and I appreciate you more than you know.

Special shout-out to the strong women who have inspired **Dawn Knight** through all her many lives – from comic book character, to website vixen, to feature film idea, to this novel in your hands. You helped shape her toughness, her softness, and her tenacity.

To **Paulara Hawkins**, who led the way and made me believe I could really do this – thank you for showing me it was possible.

To **Lisa Holly**, who helped me get so many of these ideas out of my head and onto the page – your help was clutch.

To my proofreader, who I'm sure got sick of me sending "one more" version – thank you for your patience and your eye.

To my homies that go way back and always keep it 100 – I value your honesty. When you tell me something is dope or it sucks, I believe you, and that makes me better.

To my Two Funny Mamas, for the laughs, the love, and the friendship that supports my talents.

And most of all, to *you*, the reader – thank you for spending your time, your energy, and your coins on this book. The fact that you chose to rock with my work means everything, and I hope these pages prove your trust wasn't misplaced.

DAWN KNIGHT

1 PROLOGUE – GHOST IN THE BAR

Secret government agencies had always existed, lurking in the shadows and operating under the guise of national security. The spy game never ceased; it merely evolved, shifting its focus from foreign adversaries to enemies within. Long before it stretched across borders, espionage was a local affair, entangled in the dark alleys of corruption, betrayal, and silent warfare.

Terrorism, assassination, and kidnapping were not foreign threats but homegrown afflictions festering in the marrow of the nation. Deception was not merely a strategy; it was the foundation upon which this country was built.

The air in the dimly lit room hung thick with the acrid stench of stale cigarette smoke, mingling with the sharp bite of cheap alcohol and unspoken regrets. A flickering neon sign outside the grimy window cast a sickly glow over the cracked countertop and stained floorboards. In the farthest corner, where the light barely reached, a lone figure sat hunched over a chipped glass filled with something that barely qualified as wine. She should have chosen whiskey.

A dull ache settled in her temples, a reminder of the countless nights spent drowning in the ghosts of her past. Her eyes, dark pools of unreadable depth, stared vacantly into the abyss of her thoughts. They reflected a life spent in the margins, in the places society pretended did not exist.

Corruption was no secret. The rot had seeped into every crevice of government, its stench as familiar as the smoke that curled toward the low ceiling. People no longer held faith in the system. Even those within its ranks found it difficult to stomach the hypocrisy. It was an unspoken truth, whispered in hushed conversations and painted in graffiti on crumbling city walls.

There were no more external wars—not since the world had become a singular global state—but the enemy was closer now, buried deep within. Agency clashed against agency, their secret wars waged in the dark, their conspiracies unraveling the last threads of democracy and free will. Violence no longer had a face; it was a shadow lurking in every corridor, waiting to strike.

The cities, once alive with the pulse of freedom, had become fortresses of control. Police states ruled with an iron grip, their enforcers patrolling the streets like silent sentinels. Movement was no longer a right but a privilege granted only to those who held the necessary permits and classifications. A missed curfew could mean a fate worse than imprisonment—long-term detention in the labor camps where bodies broke under the weight of endless toil.

These camps, veiled behind the pretense of justice, were nothing more than profit machines, their suffering fueling the pockets of the powerful. Global entities thrived, their wealth amassed through the backs of the oppressed, their hands gripping the levers of power through politicians and agency directors who turned blind eyes to the atrocities they enabled.

She remembered a time when the fire of patriotism burned bright within her, a belief in the greater good that had once guided her. Naïve, she had mistaken service for honor, duty for truth. That fire had long since been extinguished, smothered beneath disillusionment. Now, only a bitter cynicism remained, a taste like rusted metal on her tongue.

"I once worked for the government. I was a cog in the machine, a shadow in the endless night. But, with help from a higher source, I slipped through the cracks, vanishing back into society. Or so I thought…"

2 GENESIS – BIRTH OF GEN X (DAWN)

For years, she believed she lived anonymously. The world moved in its usual rhythm—people hurrying, the mundane chatter of everyday existence, the oblivious masses who would never know the truth. Yet, behind her calm façade, Dawn Knight harbored a past laced with shadows and blood.

Once, she had reveled in the game, believing in the cause with unshaken fervor. Women were essential—cunning, lethal, efficient—if not more so than their male counterparts. They had been through it all. Their hands just as stained, their hearts just as hardened. The propaganda had been intoxicating, molding her into the perfect soldier. When the Agency called, she answered without hesitation, eager to serve, eager to prove herself.

And then, the experiments began.

She could still recall the sterile scent of the laboratories, the metallic taste of adrenaline as the enhancements took effect. The results were staggering. They were no longer just human; they had become something more, something unnatural. The ultimate weapons. And Dawn—or A-10, as she had been designated—was among the best.

Now, she stood before her reflection, staring into a face that was both hers and not hers. The mirror revealed sharp cheekbones, full lips that could smile with deceptive warmth, and eyes that had once been alive but now bore the weight of years spent in the darkness. The woman she had become was a ghost of the girl she once was—an elite assassin sculpted for perfection, honed through ruthless training, built to seduce, infiltrate, and eliminate without hesitation.

For two decades, she had moved through the world like a phantom, slipping between the cracks of society, mingling with the rich, the corrupt, the powerful, using her allure as a weapon and her body as a tool. Each mission was another night lost in a haze of whispered secrets, clandestine meetings, and the suffocating intimacy of death.

At first, it was just a flicker of doubt—a second too long staring at a target before pulling the trigger, the quiet discomfort of bloodstains that refused to wash away. Then, hesitation turned to questions.

The names on her kill list were no longer faceless. They had lives, histories, regrets—just like her. She remembered the file of a young artist, barely twenty, whose only crime was being the nephew of a dissident leader. His sketches, confiscated by the Agency, revealed a vibrant soul, a world seen through hopeful eyes. Eyes she was supposed to extinguish.

This dissonance grew with each mission, a nagging reminder of the humanity she was forced to suppress. And suddenly, the justifications she had whispered to herself for years—this is survival, this is necessary—sounded hollow. The blood on her hands was no longer just a job requirement; it was a stain on her soul.

She questioned the Agency, its motives, the very ideals she had once lived and killed for. Was she truly serving her country, or merely a pawn in a twisted game of power and deception?

The Agency noticed her faltering loyalty. They called it a temporary breakdown, a side effect of prolonged exposure to high-risk operations. She was pulled from the field and reassigned to training recruits—a leash disguised as a promotion.

And that was when she met him.

3 LOVE AND LOSS

Professor Armitage was an enigma—a man with a God complex and a mind that blurred the lines between brilliance and madness. He was the mastermind behind the genetic experiments that had created operatives like her. He saw in Dawn a work of art, a living testament to his research. She was his finest creation, a masterpiece of destruction.

But her interest lay elsewhere. It was a recruit who caught her eye—a man who mirrored her in ways she never expected.

Matthew was different. His skill was undeniable, his drive relentless. He was her male counterpart—sharp, disciplined, and dangerous. But where she had become numb, he still held onto something pure. He still believed in the mission, in justice, in making a difference.

During a training exercise, when ordered to shoot a hostage—a simulation, of course—Matthew hesitated, his face paling. Later, he confessed to Dawn, "I couldn't do it. Even if it wasn't real, we shouldn't normalize taking innocent lives."

One evening, after a particularly grueling session, she found him alone, gazing out at the city lights, the neon glow casting sharp angles on his face. There was something in his eyes that made her pause—doubt, uncertainty, a crack in his carefully built armor.

"Rough day?" Dawn's voice was softer than usual, a quiet invitation.

Matthew didn't look at her. He kept his gaze on the city lights, his shoulders tense, his hands curled into fists. "I don't know if I can do this," he admitted. "The things they expect us to do…it goes against everything I believe."

A part of her wanted to reassure him, to say it would get easier. But that would be a lie. Instead, she sat beside him, their knees almost touching.

"I know," she murmured. "I know what it's like to carry that weight alone."

Dawn saw the conflict in Matthew's eyes—a genuine struggle between his ideals and the grim reality of their work. She knew she had to be honest with him, even if it meant revealing a part of herself she had long buried.

"Matthew," she said, her voice low, "this Agency…it will test you. It will push you to your breaking point. You have to decide what you are willing to sacrifice, what lines you won't cross, because once you do, there is no going back."

Matthew turned to face her, his gaze searching. "What about you, Dawn?"

"…Too many," she whispered. "But I try to make sure they count. Now, I will only eliminate targets that align with my moral code, not just what I'm told to do."

At last, he turned to her, something raw in his expression. "I do not want to be alone, Dawn."

She didn't either, but neither of them said it. Not yet.

For the first time in years, she allowed herself a moment of vulnerability, revealing the detachment she had built to survive. In his eyes, she saw her own struggles reflected back at her.

Their bond deepened with each passing day, their connection forged through shared battles and stolen moments of understanding. During combat drills, they moved as though connected by an unseen thread, anticipating each other's moves, a synchrony that defied logic. Instructors took note, as did the Agency.

"Don't hold back. What are you afraid of?" Dawn yelled during knife combat training.

He saw the playful excitement vanish, revealing a tone of serious competitiveness.

"These are real knives, Dawn." Knives that were almost surgically sharp.

The look in her eye said she wasn't concerned as she lunged toward him with purpose, forcing his response: counter correctly or bleed. Dawn was serious, knowing Matthew's reluctance could be a signal— the difference between life or death in the field.

Their drill evolved into an actual battle that ended with Matthew losing himself in the moment, not thinking, just reacting, no longer seeing Dawn, but an opponent looking to end him.

Dawn feinted left, her blade kissing Matthew's collarbone. His counterstrike wasn't training—it was feral instinct, the edge biting into her femoral artery. She smiled as crimson bloomed.

"Now you're learning."

Blood was drawn and the fight stopped. A deep slice cut a massive gash across Dawn's thigh.

"Oh my God! Dawn, I'm—"

She halted his apology by throwing herself into his arms.

"Congratulations."

The training ended immediately, and Matthew assisted Dawn to the infirmary, hardly able to control his emotions.

"Don't stress it," she calmly assured him. "Trust me. I'll be just fine."

But how could she be fine? There was so much blood, and he'd literally seen the muscle tissue in her leg.

That evening, guilt gnawed at him. All he could think about was how he had lost control and ruined the aesthetic perfection of Dawn's legs. And with such a deep cut, might he have damaged a nerve? He ran to her dorm room and spoke through the door.

"Dawn, I know you're laid up. I just wanted to check on you and let you know how sorry I am…fuck!"

There was motion on the other side of the door.

"Don't get up, Dawn!" he yelled in a panic.

Her dorm room door opened. "I told you not to worry about me. Stop yelling."

Matthew was stunned. She stood in front of him, completely coherent—no pain meds, no buzz from weed or alcohol, not even a limp.

"What the hell? I saw the gash! Any deeper and I would've seen your femur. Now all I see is a little scar—no stitches, not even a bandage."

A wave of dizziness washed over him as he stared at her wound. Did he imagine it? Was he tripping? The scar looked old. How long had it been there? He'd soon learn not to ask these questions out loud.

Her smile was warm and her voice reassuring. "Don't overthink it. Just know that I'm good, and you are amazing."

Within the week he had amassed a list of unbelievable things about her. It wasn't just her exceptional physicality, or how her wounds healed with unnatural swiftness, but also her aversion to giving any details about her past. But their compatibility was undeniable, and the sexual tension was thicker than refrigerated peanut butter.

One night, after another grueling training session, they walked side by side through the dimly lit corridors. The air between them was charged. Matthew stopped abruptly, turning to face her.

"I...I need to tell you something," he said, his voice betraying an unfamiliar nervousness.

Dawn's heart pounded. "What is it?"

He hesitated, then reached out, his fingers brushing against her cheek. "I have never met anyone like you," he confessed. "You're strong, intelligent...and despite everything, you still have a heart. I think...I think I'm falling for you."

This was a new experience; she felt something stir within her—something real, something both exciting and terrifying. Without a word, she leaned in, their lips meeting in a tentative, electric kiss. It was a moment of raw honesty, a silent promise, a tether between two souls lost in the same storm.

But the moment would be fleeting.

Just as she began to understand her feelings for him, the Agency intervened. He was deployed to the field before she could fully process them. With his departure, the illusion of control crumbled. They saw her as a weapon, a tool, failing to account for the human connection that had blossomed between her and Matthew. Small acts of kindness, shared glances, and whispered confidences had been dismissed as inconsequential, but they were the threads that wove a bond stronger than any programming.

The Agency had underestimated her, failing to recognize that love, once awakened, could be as powerful as hate.

That mistake would be their downfall.

The assignment had seemed routine at first—an investigation into key figures suspected of orchestrating high-profile assassinations for hire, using government resources to bolster organized crime syndicates. Like Senator Harrison Reeves, a man with a squeaky-clean public image who was secretly selling government secrets to the highest bidder. But as he delved deeper, the scope of the corruption became staggering, a malignant cancer festering within the very agencies designed to uphold justice. The rot reached the highest echelons of power, intertwining with the roots of bureaucracy, feeding off greed and deception.

He found evidence of judges accepting bribes to release dangerous criminals, politicians laundering money through offshore accounts, and agency directors manipulating intelligence to serve their own agendas. The deeper he dug, the clearer the picture became—justice was nothing more than an illusion, a well-crafted veneer to pacify the masses while the elite orchestrated their own version of order.

She had once believed in the system. Then came the Professor. He hadn't needed to persuade her. The truth had been there all along, waiting for her to open her eyes. They were sent into the world to commit unspeakable acts, not for justice, not for the greater good, but to line the pockets of those with an insatiable thirst for power.

And there was Matthew. He was everything she wasn't—idealistic, compassionate, driven by an unrelenting pursuit of true justice. His presence was like a light in the darkness, a flicker of hope amidst the moral decay that had long taken root within her. Their connection had been immediate, an unspoken understanding that transcended words. He had reminded her of the person she once was before cynicism and duty had dulled her edges, before she had surrendered to the machine that was the Agency.

She realized Matthew's idealism was a dangerous weapon, one the Agency would exploit without hesitation. She vowed to protect him, even if it meant deceiving him. She had to ensure his heart stayed pure.

"Matthew, your purity makes you the best of us."

"But I want to be like you, Dawn."

"No, you don't. Please, God…no."

Then came the call.

Matthew was dead.

The news struck like a blade, stealing her breath and shattering her illusions. She had known the ruthless nature of their profession, but this was too much. She sought answers from the Professor, hoping for reassignment to Matthew's case, but her inquiries were dismissed, shattering her belief in the system.

Matthew had represented everything she had lost—innocence, compassion, and the belief that justice could prevail. His death forced her to confront the truth: they were all disposable pieces on a board

4 THE PROFESSOR'S ASSASSIN

Her rage burned, and the Professor saw an opportunity. He coaxed her back into the field, but this mission would be different—personal. There would be no records, no oversight, only targets: figures of unimaginable influence, businessmen and politicians thriving on corruption and exploitation. The Professor, once an observer, became the puppet master, pulling strings from within the Agency as he set the stage for something greater than vengeance. He sought to dismantle the aristocracy of power, and she would be his instrument of destruction, fueled by revenge.

Her rage...repeatedly misguided.

The first wave began in blood. She moved like a ghost, slipping through shadows, leaving carnage in her wake. The assassinations were brutal, theatrical displays of violence meant to send a message. Each scene was meticulously crafted—a symphony of gore and symbolism designed to instill fear. A senator was found crucified in his office. A corporate CEO's mansion was set ablaze with him inside. A corrupt judge was dismembered, his body parts delivered to his colleagues with detailed information. Fear spread like wildfire. Governments and corporations scrambled to contain the chaos, unaware that the storm had only just begun. Each kill was precise, a macabre symphony orchestrated by the Professor, executed with an unyielding hand. She had become the nightmare they never saw coming.

Through war and peacetime, she worked, and came to understand that the world itself was governed by profit. Turmoil was not an accident—it was manufactured, the most lucrative business of all. They created monsters, building up dictators, warlords, drug lords, and presidents only to tear them down when their usefulness waned. The Agency had long lost control of its own creations. Now the monsters roamed free, serving their own ambitions.

The Agency had become something else entirely—hell. It wasn't just about espionage anymore, but control, manipulation, and the ruthless pursuit of power at any cost. The Agency had morphed into a self-serving hypocrite, its original purpose twisted beyond recognition.

Then, it was over. The Professor, meticulous as ever, arranged everything—alibis, transport, new identities. His final gift to her was freedom. He ensured her escape, severing her ties to the past so completely that she became a ghost even to those who had once controlled her.

5 FIFTEEN YEARS OF QUIET

Fifteen years passed. She had not held a gun, nor seen another's blood spilled by her hand. She had walked away from the violence, burying it beneath a new life. She ran a fitness studio, teaching others to strengthen their bodies, to find balance—a sharp contrast to the destruction she once dealt. She embraced simplicity, quiet. She was no longer just surviving; she was learning how to live.

But the past has a way of creeping back. It lingered at the edges of her mind, in the cold sweats of midnight memories. She had done terrible things. She had blood on her hands, sins that no amount of time could wash away. She told herself that she was making amends, that she was doing penance by leading a life of peace. Yet, she remained alone.

Matthew's death had stolen something vital from her. Since she walked away from the Agency, she had built walls too high for anyone to scale. She formed only the relationships necessary to maintain her façade of normalcy, never allowing anyone too close, never letting herself feel.

She had thought she was free. But freedom, like justice, was just another illusion.

And illusions always shatter.

6 COMPROMISED – THE SUITS CLOSE IN

Then, everything changed.

Fifteen years of peaceful anonymity unraveled, thread by thread, with the first unsettling phone call. It was never anything overt—just silence or the ghost of breathing before the line went dead. But she knew. And the primal instinct of being watched began to gnaw at her.

The shadows that once felt like old friends now seemed to close in, unfamiliar and menacing. She could feel the weight of unseen eyes tracking her, studying her. Waiting.

The alleyway was empty, yet Dawn could not shake the feeling of being watched. Her instincts—honed through years of survival—never lied. She shifted her stance, fingers brushing against the concealed blade in her purse. A shadow moved just out of reach, gone before she could pinpoint its source.

A trick of the light? Or something else?

The uneasy weight of familiarity gnawed at her. Someone had been there. Someone who didn't want to be seen.

She had spotted them weeks before they made their presence known. The Suits, she called them. Even in their attempts at plain clothes, they were unmistakable—their rigid posture, the methodical scanning of their surroundings, the aura of controlled detachment. Everything about them screamed government agency.

It was only a matter of time before they moved in.

Her cover had been compromised. The intricate web of lies she had spent years weaving had been torn apart by an unseen hand. Someone had found her.

The day had been long. Filled with meetings, property viewings, and discussions with potential investors, Dawn had worked tirelessly toward owning her own fitness training facility. All she wanted now was a hot bath, a glass of deep red merlot, and the sweet escape of warm, fragrant bubbles. For the first time in a while, her mind was so preoccupied with her evening plans that she let her guard slip.

She entered the parking structure, unaware that her watchers had tightened their net.

"Alpha One, team leader in position."

"10-4, Alpha One. Subject approaching your perimeter."

"Bravo Two in position."

"10-4, Bravo Two."

"Charlie Three in position."

"10-4, Charlie."

"Delta—"

A brief burst of static interrupted the transmission.

"Silence all communication. Subject approaching. Alpha One out."

As Dawn ascended the steps to her apartment, sharp, watchful eyes tracked her every movement. Tense fingers hovered near triggers. A single command could decide her fate. To them, she was just a beautiful, oblivious woman, living a life far removed from their world. But she wasn't. She never had been.

Inside, the phone rang. Balancing groceries and her purse, she fumbled with the lock, her pulse quickening. She rarely received calls, and curiosity flared. But by the time she reached the phone, the line had gone dead. A wrong number? A coincidence? She wasn't the kind of woman who believed in those.

Shaking off the unease, she turned on her laptop and headed to the bathroom, shedding the constraints of the day along with her clothes. The team continued their surveillance, their voices murmuring through comms.

"Alpha One to Bravo Two."

"Alpha One, go for Bravo Two."

"Do you have observation?"

"Affirmative, Alpha One."

She undressed, unaware—or so they thought—of the effect her lean, sculpted silhouette had on her quiet, armed spectators. They were professionals. Trained. Conditioned. But they were still men, and she was all woman. A deadly woman. The blouse came off first, revealing the taut expanse of her toned abdomen and the swell of her breasts beneath a delicate lace bra. Next, she peeled off the tight pants that clung to her long, powerful legs, leaving only the whisper of a skimpy mesh bikini and bra against her skin.

She poured herself a glass of merlot and pressed play on her stereo. The soft strains of jazz filled the apartment, its low, sultry hum a contrast to the tension coiling in her gut. She exhaled, willing herself to relax, but the sensation of being watched had settled in like an unshakable chill. The phone rang again.

Two rings. Then silence.

Frowning, she snatched up the device. Another missed call.

Something was wrong.

Her gaze flicked to the large picture window. Normally, she left the blinds open. After all, she lived high enough that no one could see in. But tonight, the hair on her arms stood on end. Slowly, deliberately, she pulled the blinds shut.

"Alpha One to Bravo Two."

"Bravo Two, move in."

"I've lost visual on the subject. Do you have surveillance?"

"Negative. No visual."

Inside, oblivious to their scrambling, Dawn sank into the warm embrace of her bath.

Yet even in her sanctuary, her senses remained attuned, honed from years of survival. Something felt off.

After her bath, she moved to her desk, still wrapped in the glow of candlelight, her bare skin drying in the air. As she scanned her emails, a familiar name stopped her cold.

The Professor.

It had been years since their last contact, but the message was clear. The code was simple enough to decipher:

Hello. Long time no chat. Hope all is well with you. Let's do lunch.

Translation: Dawn, your cover and location have been compromised.

Ice slithered down her spine. Instinct took over. The fitness instructor disappeared, and in her place, the assassin was reborn. The seamless transition was terrifying in its efficiency. Every muscle in her body coiled with lethal intent.

She stood, walking toward the blinds, feigning a casual glance at the view while her sharp eyes sought out the watchers. She knew exactly how this would end. The only question was: did she want to play along?

From their vantage point, they saw nothing but a stunning woman, her bare skin illuminated by city lights, stretching, arching—an image of effortless seduction. But she knew better, knew what their distraction meant, knew how many seconds she had left before the breach.

"Alpha One, copy. Moving in. Discontinue all transmission until you receive my signal."

She had prepared for this. A packed bag in the closet. Money, travel papers, a gun, and extra ammo. She could vanish in minutes. But the thought of running again, of starting over, filled her with a deep, burning resentment.

Maybe this time, she wouldn't run.

Maybe this time, she would fight.

The clock was ticking. The door would be breached at any moment.

Her first instinct was to face them naked—let the shock buy her a precious moment. But she needed to be ready. Slipping into her underwear, she yanked on a pair of jeans, a fitted T-shirt, and heavy boots just as the front door slowly, ominously creaked open.

She exhaled.

Game on.

7 A Dead Man at the Door

A small bell chimed, slicing through the silence like a knife. The sound sent a ripple of alarm through Dawn, her senses sharpening as adrenaline surged through her veins. Her mind dissected the moment in slow motion—the door creaking open, a shadow slipping inside, and then the cold gleam of a gun barrel, a harbinger of danger, piercing through the dim light.

The figure moved cautiously, steps calculated, intent uncertain.

Dawn reacted instinctively, reaching for the gun nestled in her nightstand. With practiced ease, she leveled the weapon, her breath steady as she locked onto the door, poised for the inevitable confrontation.

"Dawn, don't shoot!"

The voice struck her like lightning, jolting her instincts and allowing hesitation to creep in. It was a rare mistake—one that could cost her life. Hesitation was weakness, a flaw she had long since eradicated, yet something in the familiarity and resonance of that voice made her pause.

The figure stepped further into the room, hands raised in surrender, his face now visible in the slivers of moonlight filtering through the blinds.

"It can't be," she whispered, her voice barely audible.

Her grip tightened around the gun, her mind warring between reality and illusion.

"It's me, Dawn. I'm alive. We don't have time. I'll explain later."

"Matthew…"

Her heart pounded, her pulse roaring. This was a trick. It had to be. The Agency had pulled worse stunts. She took a slow, deliberate step forward, her gun unwavering, her eyes scanning for any detail that could betray the deception.

"Tell me something," she said, her voice low and edged with steel. It was not a request, but a test.

If this was truly Matthew, he would understand. He would know exactly what she meant.

"You have a beauty mark shaped like a heart on your inner left thigh…"

She narrowed her eyes, a blush rising despite the gravity of the situation. "I'm standing here in my drawers. You could've seen it."

He tilted his head slightly, a smirk ghosting across his lips, his eyes locking on hers with an intensity that made her breath hitch.

"You like to have it licked…slowly."

Her breath hitched. The gun wavered.

"Matthew…"

She lowered her weapon, but the battle within her was far from over.

A tidal wave of emotions crashed into her—relief, disbelief, longing. She wanted to reach out, to touch him, to confirm that he was real, but there was no time.

"Come on! We have to go."

She understood the urgency, grabbing her go-bag from beneath the bed. The pieces weren't fitting together, but she trusted her instincts enough to know staying wasn't option. Between the Professor's cryptic message and Matthew's reappearance, one thing was clear—she was a target.

They had barely cleared the bedroom before the windows shattered, shards of glass catching the moonlight like deadly stars. Canisters clattered against the floor, spewing thick clouds of gas, their acrid tendrils seeping into the air, clawing at her lungs. The living room door burst open, a battering ram of force, and then they were upon them—black-clad operatives, their movements precise, their intent clear.

Sometimes you fight. Sometimes you run.

But tonight, the choice was not theirs to make.

The first operative lunged, but Dawn was faster. She pivoted, twisted, and delivered a precise strike to the throat—he went down. Matthew moved like a specter beside her, disarming and disabling with calculated movements—a dance of destruction.

For a moment, it was as if they were back in training, back in the field, the thrill of combat thrumming through their veins. They fought with the synchronicity of old partners, their bodies attuned to each other in a deadly ballet. One by one, the agents fell, their mission to capture her unraveling.

"Hallway. Now." Matthew's voice was clipped, controlled.

Dawn didn't need to be told twice. They sprinted down the corridor, feet pounding against the floor, breath coming in sharp bursts. The stairwell was their only option. The elevator was a death trap.

"I've been watching you for days," Matthew said, taking the steps two at a time. Despite the situation, he barely sounded winded. "So have they."

Her mind raced, a sliver of doubt flashing through. A sliver of hesitation.

"You mean to protect me," she uttered, her voice barely audible, "or to trap me?"

The question hung in the air, thick with years of betrayal and uncertainty. Could she truly trust him? Or was he just another pawn in a game she didn't understand?

Matthew's expression flickered, a shadow passing over his face. "Does it matter, Dawn? Either way, you're with me now."

His words didn't fully quell her doubts, but they were enough to keep her moving, to keep her fighting. She knew she had to trust someone, and right now, Matthew was all she had.

Dawn remained focused, locked on the descent. Fifteen flights. The number was daunting, but better than the alternative.

"You remember the procedure for bag and grab?" he asked, a challenge in his voice.

Dawn shot him a look. "It's like riding a bike."

"How many agents?"

"Eight now. There were twelve." He grinned as they stepped over one of his casualties. "They're a little light. Maybe we should wait for backup. After all, they're after Gen X, Agent 10."

The name sent a shiver down her spine. It had been years since she had been Gen X, but it did not matter. The training, the instincts—they never left. She might have been Dawn Knight, civilian, but at her core, she was still a weapon.

***

Snagging a pair of night-vision goggles and a radio from a fallen agent, she fell into old habits seamlessly. Matthew noticed, his admiration unspoken but palpable.

"Where's the car?" she asked, adjusting the headset.

"West. Off the alley."

They hit ground level, their pace never faltering. The Agency had miscalculated. They had assumed Dawn was soft, that time had dulled her edge. But as she slid into the passenger seat of the nondescript black hybrid, she knew one thing for certain—

They had made a grave mistake.

The engine roared to life, and within moments, they disappeared into the night, leaving chaos in their wake.

8 Hiding in Plain Sight – Motel Confessions

The motel smelled of stale air and cleaning supplies—a building easily forgotten, nestled between a truck stop and a row of abandoned shops.

The neon vacancy sign flickered against the darkness, humming softly in the silence. The room was passable—clean but devoid of personality—with beige walls, a worn bed, and a window covered by thin, tattered blinds that barely concealed the world outside. It was exactly what Dawn needed: inconspicuous enough to disappear.

She had learned early that hiding in plain sight was often the best strategy. No need for dingy, crime-infested motels with peeling wallpaper and ominous stains. A decent, middle-of-the-road lodge was perfect. And traveling with Matthew in a hybrid? The perfect cover—they looked like any other young couple on a road trip: unremarkable, forgettable.

Once inside, she secured the room with practiced ease, scanning for threats before locking the door. The moment the deadbolt clicked, she turned on Matthew, fury radiating off her like a heatwave.

"What the fuck was that about?" Dawn's voice cut through the air like a blade, low but sharp enough to wound. "How did you find me, Matthew? And how did they?"

Matthew met her glare but didn't flinch. "I had to get to you first," he said, measured. "Just listen—"

"Fuck that," she snapped. "I'm done listening to lies."

He exhaled, his jaw tightening. "You have no idea what they—"

"No," she interrupted, stepping closer, her voice now a whisper. "You have no idea how many times I've been betrayed."

Silence stretched between them.

"So tell me," she continued, watching his every breath, "should I add you to the list?"

Matthew remained composed, but urgency threaded his words. "Dawn, I swear, I was never your enemy."

"You lied to me." Her voice was sharp, but beneath it, something raw.

He raked a hand across his head. "I had no choice."

"You always had a choice," she shot back. "You just chose them over me."

Silence. A muscle ticked in his jaw.

"That's not true." His voice was quieter now, rough with something dangerously close to regret. "I chose you every damn time. You just didn't know it."

Her breath hitched. "All these years…I thought you were dead. I had no idea you were alive. I need to process this." Her voice wavered, her usually steely demeanor cracking under the weight of old wounds. "I never wanted to believe you were dead. For so long, I felt dead inside. So cold."

Matthew crossed the room in an instant, closing the distance between them. His arms wrapped around her—strong, familiar, intoxicating.

"I couldn't come to you," he whispered against her hair. "It was to keep you safe. It was for the best."

Their bodies aligned as if no time had passed. The years, the pain, the questions—all melted in the presence of raw need. There were no more words, only the heat of their touch, the desperate way they undressed one another. It wasn't gentle; it was urgent, devouring, years of longing compressed into moments. They took what they needed, grasping at lost time, their bodies clashing with a hunger that burned away everything else.

When the urgency ebbed, the real reunion began. It was slower, deeper, a rekindling of something that had never truly died. They moved together in rhythm, reclaiming each other, erasing the years of distance with every whispered breath and lingering touch.

When dawn broke, sunlight streamed through the blinds, cutting the dim room into slanted streaks of gold and shadow. Clothes were scattered across the floor, evidence of a night spent unraveling and remaking themselves. They lay tangled in the sheets, bodies warm, minds restless.

Dawn stirred first, her voice barely a whisper. "All these years, I thought you were dead. Did you ever think about me?"

Matthew ran a hand through her hair, his fingers tracing its silkiness. "Every single day. But I couldn't come to you. It was too dangerous."

"Dangerous for who? You or me?"

"For both of us…" He hesitated, a warning in the pause. "We can never let the Professor know what happened last night. He's always been…possessive of you, Dawn. If he knows we're together, he'll use it against us. He can't be trusted."

Dawn stiffened. "Why?"

"The Professor has a way of manipulating things, tilting the scales to his advantage."

Her eyes narrowed. "Is he behind this? Why would he blow my cover?"

"I don't know for sure, but it's possible." He exhaled heavily, the weight of a secret pressing against him. "I know he's obsessed with you. He always has been."

Dawn sat up, her bare skin illuminated by the creeping daylight. "What?"

Matthew hesitated, then delivered the truth. "When he looks at you, he sees a lot more than an agent. He doesn't look at you as a manager, mentor, or handler."

Dawn felt the air thicken, her heart hammering against her ribs. "That's insane."

"Is it? You're not naïve, Dawn. You were trained to read people. We both know the protocols for some of the 'do whatever is necessary' assignments."

The words felt like a scalpel cutting through her chest—precise, deliberate, merciless.

"So what does that mean?"

"Do I have to spell it out? Let's not insult our intelligence." Slightly frustrated, he continued, "You manipulate men's feelings...so you aren't oblivious to his attraction to you."

"What do you expect me to say that wouldn't insult you?" Dawn's response was just as sharp. "Let's stop here before this conversation gets weird."

"It's already weird..." Matthew reached to embrace her, but she pulled away.

Further words went unspoken; silence seemed best. Some secrets should be kept...for now.

Matthew exited the room, the outside air refreshing. He looked around cautiously for signs of abnormal activity. His preliminary scan faltered as an uncomfortable, long-repressed memory surfaced.

He could hear the Professor's voice:

"Genetic imprinting is an amazing thing. They say generational traumas can be passed on. I wonder if the same holds true for emotional connections. Attraction. Love?"

9 Matthew's Manufactured Childhood

Matthew stood confused, wondering why he'd been summoned, what the play was. But he had learned early on to hold his tongue, never question. There was always a method to the madness perpetuated by the man who, since Matthew's earliest memory, had never allowed him to call him anything other than Professor.

Matthew was torn; he both loved and loathed the Professor. As he matured, love waned.

"You never knew your mother, Matthew. She was an amazing woman. I loved her so much. When she was taken from me..." His confession faltered as, for the first time, a crack in his cold demeanor revealed emotion. "I separated you from Dawn to protect you, Matthew—to protect both of you."

Anger welled up, everything Matthew had been holding in bubbling to the surface. So many questions. Why?

"Dawn's part of my research, aspects of a project created for the Agency... She is a clone... she is your mother's clone."

Matthew recoiled as if struck, his face draining of color. His breath hitched, his mind reeling. The world tilted on its axis, throwing everything he thought he knew into chaos. The room spun, the Professor's words echoing like a death knell. He stumbled backward, hand flying to his mouth, bile rising.

"You're lying!" he spat.

The truth sat in his chest like a lead weight, suffocating him. Every moment he had spent with Dawn—every kiss, every touch—had it all been some sick experiment? Some twisted recreation of the past?

"You knew," Matthew finally said, his voice hoarse. "You let this happen."

The Professor steepled his fingers. "I created her to be perfect. Like Evelyn, the woman I loved—your mother. You see why you were drawn to her."

Matthew surged to his feet, fists clenching. "She's not Evelyn."

"No," the Professor agreed, rising slowly. "She is something more."

Matthew turned and stormed out, bile rising again. How could he face Dawn knowing what she was? Knowing his feelings for her? Were they real or—as the Professor suggested—genetic imprinting?

10 CREATION – THE PROFESSOR'S MASTERPIECE

They say the line between genius and madness is thin. If true, it was surely drawn with Dr. Alistair Armitage in mind, the man known only as "The Professor." His brilliance was undeniable, his intellect unparalleled, yet a darkness lurked beneath the surface—an obsession threatening to consume him. The Agency knew of his exploits but couldn't have imagined it would come to this.

An enigma even among those who thrived in the shadows, he was a figure of legend—mysterious, all-knowing, with an almost supernatural ability to predict outcomes. Some likened him to the Wizard of Oz, an unseen puppet master pulling the strings of fate, orchestrating events few could comprehend.

Yet, for all his intellect and power, he had one fatal flaw—love. To him, love wasn't connection but weakness, a vulnerability to be exploited, manipulated, and ultimately destroyed. It was a dangerous variable in his carefully calculated world.

Her name was Evelyn Reed, and she was the crack in his armor. Their love had been a secret, a dangerous and passionate affair defying the cold, calculated world they inhabited. He met her in Berlin, during what should have been a routine operation. But Evelyn was anything but routine. Where Alistair was meticulous and methodical, she was impulsive, driven by instinct and fire. Her smile was a weapon, sharp and disarming, capable of unraveling even the most stoic of men.

And unravel him, she did.

Their time together consisted of stolen moments, whispers in the dark, heated exchanges in dimly lit safe houses. Theirs was a love built on adrenaline, knowing every kiss could be their last, every meeting could end in betrayal or bloodshed. But for Alistair, it was more than just passion—it was a rebirth. Evelyn awakened something in him, a conscience he had long buried beneath layers of cynicism and obedience. She wanted out, wanted more than a life dictated by orders and classified files. And because he loved her, he wanted that too.

For her, he began to question the Agency, to peer beneath its noble façade. What he found was a rot spreading to the highest levels of global power—politicians, corporate magnates, and war profiteers who wielded the Agency as their private tool for controlling markets and conflicts. It was Evelyn's investigation, however, that unearthed the full extent of the corruption. She uncovered enough evidence to bring them down, enough to shake the world to its core. But she had no idea how dangerous her knowledge had made her.

Unaware she was already trapped, she planned her escape. She didn't tell Alistair about the pregnancy, wanting to wait until they were safe—though safety was an illusion in their world.

That night, rain washed over the city in heavy sheets. Evelyn stayed late at the Agency, tying off loose ends before disappearing. She knew she was being watched and had grown accustomed to the game, but this time, the game had changed.

She sensed them before she saw them—shadowy figures in her periphery as she stepped onto the rain-slicked pavement. Heart hammering, she reached for her phone, dialing the one number she knew by heart: Alistair. It rang twice, then went dead as she reached the underpass.

The impact was sudden and violent—the screech of tires, blinding headlights, the force that sent her car careening into the concrete barrier. It looked like an accident, but it wasn't. The world faded as her blood mixed with the rain, pooling across shattered glass and twisted metal.

Alistair waited for her call that night, as always. When his phone remained silent, unease settled in his gut. Then came the chilling message from a contact in the police department:

"Car crash. Underpass. It's her."

He barely remembered the drive to the hospital, his mind a storm of denial and fury. He arrived to find her motionless, a fragile, broken figure among the wires and tubes keeping her alive. Then the doctors delivered the unthinkable: Evelyn was carrying his child, a son— Matthew.

Alistair Armitage, the man who had always been three steps ahead, who had spent his life outmaneuvering the most dangerous players in the world, had failed to protect the one thing that mattered most.

As he stood over her, grief and rage coiled around his soul like a tightening noose. "It wasn't an accident," he hissed to a sympathetic colleague. "They silenced her." Whoever was responsible had just made the gravest mistake of their lives.

Consumed by loss, Alistair dedicated himself to genetic research, seeking to defy death and control life itself. The Twenty Project, initially aimed at regenerative medicine—a means to prolong life and mend what was once considered irreparable—evolved into the creation of humanoids: cloning. Grief twists even the most righteous pursuits, and for the Professor, his loss birthed an obsession that would forever alter the course of scientific ethics.

As Evelyn's life hung in the balance, the Professor's focus shifted from innovation to desperation. Consumed by anguish, his brilliance curdled into madness. The sterile, fluorescent halls of the hospital became his second home, yet he didn't linger in waiting rooms or find solace in the steady beeping of life-support machines. Instead, he turned to his private laboratory, abandoning protocol and forsaking the Agency's official research facilities in favor of secrecy. He stole samples of her DNA, harvesting what he could in the hope of saving her. In the name of love, he defied nature.

The experiments began with a single goal: to create a serum that could regenerate Evelyn's failing organs long enough for the fetus she carried to survive. But in the process, he stumbled upon something far greater—a discovery that led to the creation of the Gen series hybrids. Each bore traces of her genetic code, a haunting testament to the woman he could not save.

The early results were monstrous. Gens One through Eight were riddled with defects—grotesque and unstable—their very existence a testament to the imperfections of early creation. But then came Nine through Twenty. These specimens were different. They were perfect. And lethal.

The Professor had broken laws, defied ethics, and abandoned his own humanity. Yet the Agency—ever pragmatic, ever opportunistic— saw the potential in his work. They turned a blind eye to his transgressions, covering them up, erasing the evidence of his failures. They let him continue under one condition: the creations belonged to them.

Gens Ten through Twenty were no longer mere scientific marvels; they were weapons. Groomed to serve the government, they were sculpted into shadows, assassins as silent as whispers, as deadly as legend. They were ghosts, sent into the world to infiltrate and eliminate without question or hesitation. Few outside the Agency knew of their existence. Fewer still understood the full extent of what had been accomplished. Even the Gens themselves were oblivious to their origins.

Memory implants ensured their allegiance. Fabricated lives were woven into their subconscious, directing, shaping, molding them into the perfect operatives. It was no wonder Dawn Knight had no inkling of what she truly was—just another recruit, another gifted asset drawn into the Agency's fold.

Or so she believed.

Within the Agency's labyrinthine halls, whispers circulated about the Professor's unorthodox methods and the Twenty Project. Some saw him as a visionary, pushing the boundaries of science for national security. Others viewed him with suspicion, fearing his unchecked ambition and the ethical implications of his work.

Agent Sterling Price, a high-ranking official known for his rigid adherence to protocol, had long harbored doubts about the Professor's activities. "Armitage operates outside our authority," he confided to a trusted colleague. "His creations are weapons, and weapons must be controlled. We cannot allow him to play God without oversight."

Price suspected the Professor was not planning to destroy the aristocracy, but to become it. Little did the Agency know that time was quickly approaching.

Each Gen had been designed with a distinct identity—a set of character traits tailored to their roles. But Dawn was different. She was more than an asset. She was the Professor's masterpiece, his prize.

She was seduction and danger entwined, a lethal combination of beauty and death. She was Mata Hari reborn, Shalimar in flesh and blood—a siren who lured her prey in with honeyed whispers before striking with the precision of a viper. Driven by grief and vengeance, the Professor had created her with unparalleled skill, pouring into her every ounce of knowledge, every perfected technique.

The Agency believed Gen Ten through Twenty were equals, each possessing their own strengths. But the truth was far more unsettling.

Gen Ten—Dawn—was more than advanced. She was superior, yet also more vulnerable. Her senses were sharper, her reflexes faster, her body stronger, her regenerative abilities far exceeding the others, yet each strength came with a price. Her enhanced metabolism made her more susceptible to toxins, and her emotional capacity made her vulnerable to manipulation.

The Professor kept this truth hidden, safeguarding his precious creation from the prying eyes of those who would seek to control her even more than they already did. He knew that to control Dawn, he had to allow her to believe she was in control, even as he subtly guided her actions.

The Gens were never permitted to meet one another, their lives carefully isolated to prevent the possibility of shared knowledge. Each was awakened in solitude, conditioned to believe their path was their own. They trained in silence, each session tailored to their unique abilities and missions. They mastered languages, honed their skills in deception, and became fluent in reading the unspoken language of the human body. Every glance, every twitch of muscle, every shift in weight—these subtle signals could betray a lie before words were ever spoken. Understanding and manipulating these silent cues became the foundation of their success.

And in this, as in all things, Dawn excelled.

To her, deception was not a skill but an instinct—a second nature. It came as easily as breathing, as naturally as the beat of her heart. That was what made her dangerous. That was what made her the best.

She was more than just the Professor's most prized experiment. She was his legacy, his vengeance—a beautiful, alluring package of seduction and slaughter. And if he had his way, she would change the world in ways neither the Agency nor the government could ever predict.

Twist. A sub-basement. The smell...changes.

***

SINS OF THE FATHER

Matthew grew up in the Professor's shadow, a lonely boy raised in a world of secrets and lies. Alistair, consumed by his work and haunted by Evelyn's memory, struggled to connect with his son. He believed love was a weakness, a vulnerability to be exploited, and kept Matthew at arm's length—a subject of observation rather than affection.

Dr. Alistair Armitage—the Professor—had forbidden Matthew to call him father, forcing distance by only allowing Matthew to refer to him as "Professor," cultivating a complex relationship of love and loathing. Matthew yearned for a connection, a glimpse into the man behind the cold façade. He devoured books, seeking answers to questions the Professor refused to acknowledge, and saw the haunted look in Alistair's eyes, sensing the unspoken grief that permeated their existence.

"Tell me about my mother," Matthew pleaded one day, his voice trembling with desperate hope.

The Professor's face darkened. "Your mother's a ghost, Matthew. Best left undisturbed."

As Matthew matured under the vestige of the Agency, he witnessed firsthand the corruption and moral compromises within. This fueled his idealism, and joining the Agency's elite became his objective.

"I want to protect people," he declared, his eyes shining with fervor. "I want to make sure what happened to my mother never happens again."

The Professor merely nodded, a flicker of something unreadable in his gaze. "Very well, Matthew. But remember, the world is not as black and white as you believe. Prepare yourself for the shades of grey."

Little did Matthew know, he was walking into a world where the lines between good and evil were blurred beyond recognition—a world where his own father was a master of manipulation, and where the woman he would come to love was a creation born of grief and vengeance.

11 The Summoning – Dawn and the Professor's Forbidden Intimacy

The Professor's Office

The warm glow of the fireplace cast flickering shadows across the sprawling mahogany desk, the scent of aged whiskey mixing with the ever-present musk of cigar smoke. The Professor's office was more than a workspace—it was a sanctum, a domain of knowledge and control. Every book, every artifact had a purpose, just like the people in his world.

Dawn stood by the massive window, gazing at the city below, her reflection ghosting against the glass. She wasn't sure how she had ended up here tonight—only that she never said no when he summoned her. Was it fear? Obedience? Or something darker, something she didn't want to admit?

She should have been training, refining the skills he had so carefully cultivated, but instead, she was here again.

"You are restless tonight." His voice was a whisper against her ear, his presence behind her as solid and inescapable as the Agency's steel walls.

Dawn shivered, hating her body's reaction to him. "You shouldn't have called me here," she said, her voice steadier than she felt.

"And yet, you came." His fingers brushed her wrist, deliberate, testing.

She swallowed hard, her pulse betraying her. "I had no choice."

He chuckled, dark amusement in his tone. "Haven't we long abandoned the illusion of choice, my dear?" His fingers trailed higher, along her throat. "We are what we were designed to be."

Dawn closed her eyes. Was that true? Had she ever had agency in this…whatever this was? Had he sculpted her desire as carefully as he had sculpted her training?

"You think I'm a puppet."

The Professor shifted, turning her to face him, his pale eyes piercing her defenses. "Not a puppet. My masterpiece."

She should have resisted. She should have walked away. But when his lips claimed hers, she surrendered—as she always had.

12 CLONE REVELATION

The inevitable had arrived as Dawn and Matthew unpacked all that had transpired. The Agency wanted her back by any means. The Professor, playing both sides, had orchestrated the elaborate ruse, using Matthew as a pawn, knowing he had been surveilling her. Emotion often wins over logic when the heart cries out.

It was a simple matter of connecting the dots and selling the plan, because the Professor needed Dawn as much as the Agency did.

So did Matthew.

He paced the small room, his mind a whirlwind of conflict. He had to tell her, had to make her understand why he had pulled away.

When Dawn entered, he turned sharply. "We need to talk."

She hesitated. "About what?"

He exhaled, running a hand through his hair. "About you. About what you are."

Her expression tightened. "What are you talking about?"

Matthew's chest ached. "You're Evelyn's clone."

Dawn stilled, the words hitting her like a physical blow. "That's not—"

"It's the truth." His voice cracked. "And I didn't know how to tell you."

She backed away, her breath unsteady. Everything inside her fractured. Her hands trembled. "Then what are we, Matthew?"

He looked at her, anguish in his eyes. "I don't know."

The silence between them was deafening, an abyss neither knew how to cross.

Matthew watched her, his mind racing. This wasn't the reaction he had expected—no panic, no breakdown, just quiet acceptance.

Was she in shock? Or was this simply how clones reacted to devastating revelations? He wasn't sure. So he said nothing, simply observing as she ate, as if nothing earth-shattering had just unfolded.

But beneath the calm exterior, Dawn's mind was spinning, calculating. The revelation of her origins had shaken her, but she refused to crumble. If she had been designed, then perhaps she could redesign herself. Perhaps this was not the end of her story, but the beginning of something far greater.

One thing was certain—she would no longer be the Professor's puppet. And she would uncover the truth, no matter the cost.

TRUTH

Dawn stared at her reflection in the dimly lit motel bathroom, her dark eyes scanning the mirror for answers buried beneath her skin. The fluorescent light flickered overhead, casting a ghostly glow against the cracked tiles. The revelation gnawed at her, clawing through her mind with insidious persistence—she was a clone. Not a daughter, not a sister, not even a person born of flesh and blood as she had once believed, but a construct, a carefully designed instrument of death, created in a lab for a purpose beyond her choosing.

The knowledge didn't devastate her. It merely confirmed what she had long suspected.

She had always known she was different. It wasn't just her exceptional physicality, the way her body refused to age at a normal pace, how her wounds healed with unnatural swiftness, or how she moved with an effortless lethality others in the field could only envy. It was something deeper: the absence of hesitation, the void where guilt and morality should have lived. Why could she kill without remorse? Why could she silence a life as easily as one flicked off a light switch?

The answer was now irrefutable: she had no conscience because she was never meant to have one. It simply wasn't bred into her.

The Professor had ensured that. He had sculpted her, molded her, engineered her down to the finest detail. Every reaction, every instinct, every carefully calculated movement—it all traced back to him.

And yet, despite the artificiality of her existence, she still felt. The weight of memory, the echoes of love and loss—were they nothing more than pre-programmed responses? Or was there something more?

She clenched her fists, her reflection staring back at her, her own eyes searching for the answer.

She exhaled sharply, fogging the mirror for a moment before the glass cleared again, revealing her face—unchanged, un-aged, a deception unto itself. Her memories, the childhood she had clung to, the parents she had loved, the tender warmth of her first love—all of it was an illusion, a fabrication crafted by the very hands that had sculpted her into the perfect weapon. Every laugh, every tear, every whispered promise—lies, woven seamlessly into her consciousness to shape her into what they needed.

Dawn turned from the mirror and slipped back into the darkened room. Beyond the heavy curtains, the city hummed, neon light bleeding through the cracks and washing the space in eerie colors. The bed creaked under Matthew's sleeping weight, his breath slow and steady. She watched him, arms crossed, her silhouette framed by the sliver of light from the bathroom.

Matthew. The only man she had ever loved—if love was even something she was capable of. The memories of him felt real, tangible, despite the truth of her existence. But could she trust them? Could she trust him? His presence was both a comfort and a complication. He had returned like a resurrected ghost, carrying his own secrets. Had he been another piece of the Professor's grand design, another cog in her artificial life? Or had he, like her, been forced into a role he hadn't chosen?

She inhaled deeply, letting his scent settle into her senses. None of it mattered now. Whether her past—or Matthew—was a lie, she had one purpose left: survival. The Agency had summoned her back, and though it was the last thing she envisioned, she would do what was necessary. If survival meant taking their orders once more, then so be it.

She wasn't ready to die.

Clone or not, Dawn intended to live.

13 INTO THE OUTER WORLD

The world was split in two—divided by towering walls of steel, concrete, and the cold calculations of those who deemed themselves superior. On one side, the Secure Cities: polished skyscrapers kissed by artificial sunlight, streets humming with automated traffic, and an unyielding order that kept the privileged cocooned in their illusion of safety.

On the other, the Outer World: a vast, decaying wasteland where the forgotten clawed for survival amid the ruins of a past civilization.

Only a select few dared to traverse the abyss between these realms— tech workers under armed escort, penal enforcement officers hardened by years of patrolling the fringes, and those whose fate had already been sealed. The journey from the artificial paradise of a Secure City to the fractured reality beyond was more than a passage through physical space—it was a slow unraveling of the grand illusion, a descent into a world where human suffering had been swept under the rug of progress.

Exiting the Secure City was no simple feat. Gates of reinforced titanium loomed, monitored by biometric scans, DNA sampling, and a complex algorithm that determined who could pass. Each checkpoint, each mechanical voice confirming authorization, felt like another chain tightening around those forced to leave. The walls were more than barriers; they were a final, suffocating embrace meant to keep the horrors of the Outer World at bay. Yet, despite the city's rigid control, cracks existed—thin fractures through which human vice seeped.

Beyond the gates, black markets thrived in the shadows of the slums. Whispers of illicit trade echoed against crumbling brick walls—contraband technology, human lives bartered like cattle, weapons exchanged under broken neon signs. The Outer World had built its own brutal hierarchy where only the ruthless survived. But Dawn's mission lay beyond these underworld dealings, her purpose far greater than anything street merchants and traffickers could offer.

The Professor had arranged everything. Her cover was simple: a correspondent documenting "a night in the life" of Secure City's security forces. A shift supervisor, carefully selected and well-compensated for his silence, would be her guide, providing access to restricted city schematics and leading her through hidden underground passages that snaked beneath the surface. At the end of this path awaited her destination—an old, condemned government facility, forgotten by most but harboring a truth powerful enough to fracture the world.

Dawn tightened her grip on her case, feeling the cold steel beneath her fingers ground her. This was no mere act of rebellion, no reckless attempt at uncovering buried secrets. The Professor had given her a reason, a promise of answers—proof that her existence was more than that of a tool, a weapon forged for a war she had never agreed to fight. The path ahead was perilous, but she had no choice.

As the towering structures of the Secure City faded, swallowed by the darkness of the Outer World, she felt the weight of inevitability. This was the cost of progress. The Secure Cities had not eradicated suffering—they had merely pushed it beyond their borders, letting it fester in the shadows. Dawn took a deep breath, steeling herself.

The abyss awaited, and she was ready to descend.

Five hours earlier, in a generic city, Dawn stood on a high-rise balcony, surveying the metropolis. Since the Union's formation, cities had become mere copies—monolithic grids of steel and glass, their streets awash with the same gaudy neon signs advertising corporate brands, fast food, and disposable fashion. Stripped of individuality, they had become sterile, lifeless shells that masked the decay beneath. She could have been in any Secure City; only subtle differences in street-sign dialects and slight architectural variations distinguished them. But that was not why she was here.

The Secure City gleamed under artificial lights, a utopia built on the illusion of order. Towering steel spires stretched toward the sky, mirrored surfaces reflecting a false world. The air smelled of sterilized perfection, a controlled, manufactured peace.

But beyond its borders, the façade crumbled. The Outer World was a festering wound beneath the city's skin—a place where the forgotten roamed, where neon dreams turned to rust. The streets outside the walls reeked of decay, old fires smoldering in the distance. Here, power wasn't dictated by government mandates but by the weight of one's weapon.

The city's elite never looked beyond the walls. They didn't have to.

Outside, the world teetered on the brink of extinction, a realm where madness reigned and the desperate were left to fend for themselves. In these lawless zones, the impoverished became prey, and civilization was a distant memory.

It had been too long since Dawn last ventured beyond the walls, and she had nearly forgotten how far one had to travel to reach the fringes. The shuttles that ferried people in and out of the Secure City were restricted to civil servants, city security, maintenance workers, and Outer World Transporters—individuals who knew the truth behind the illusion. These silent gatekeepers maintained the underground system of corruption, orchestrating the secret movements of people, goods, and forbidden knowledge. They controlled the covert tunnels, determined the rules of the gangs, and profited from the flow of contraband, narcotics, and information. The corruption ran deep, an unspoken contract between the law and the lawless, acknowledged only in whispers by those who profited.

The Professor's plan was precise. Dawn would take the tunnels—three condemned buildings, each serving a purpose. The first, crowded but secure. The second, long forgotten. The third, on the city's edge, barely standing.

Through these ruins, she would reach the Outer World. Her cover as a reporter held, and her background check cleared. Her contact, a sympathetic insider, would ensure she had a four-hour window before the next security sweep—all the time she needed to reach the installation. It was a long-forgotten government facility buried beneath the wasteland, rumored to house grotesque secret experiments. There, in the depths of a hidden laboratory, she would find proof of the Professor's claim: the second phase of the 100 Project and the mutations it had birthed.

Feigning exhaustion from travel, Dawn had requested privacy to review her notes. The shift supervisor, indifferent to her presence, granted her access to a small sleeping quarter and handed over a security briefing that included the facility's layout. At precisely 04:00, she moved. Slipping into the dimly lit corridors, she moved with practiced precision, her pulse steady, senses on high alert. The stairwells and hallways matched her memorization, each turn bringing her closer to the basement. Hidden among the ordinary ventilation systems and maintenance access points were the signs she sought—faint markings that led to the secret passages known only to those who trafficked in shadows.

She located an air duct, its metal grille loosened by years of neglect. With practiced ease, she pried it open and slipped inside, the cold steel pressing against her skin as she crawled through the narrow shaft. The Professor had equipped her with specialized sunglasses—more than a mere accessory; they functioned as a two-way visual device, allowing her to scan her surroundings and relay real-time footage to her navigator.

The moment she descended into the underground tunnels, her communicator crackled to life.

"Dawn, do you read me?" The voice was distorted, breaking with static, but she recognized it.

"I read you. Signal is weak, but I'm moving forward."

Her navigator attempted to guide her, but the interference worsened the deeper she went. The darkness pressed in, the cold air thick with the scent of damp earth and rusting metal. Panic threatened, but she forced it down, relying on memory, on the maps she had studied for days. The corridors were labyrinthine, each turn identical. Her breath was steady; her heartbeat quickened.

Then, suddenly, the navigator's voice broke through the static.

"You're close. Fifty yards ahead. There's an exit. Once you're out, head west—thirty-five blocks."

She nodded, though he could not see her, and pressed on. The tunnel opened to a corroded service hatch barely clinging to its hinges. She forced it open and stepped out into the night. The air was thick with decay and the sharp scent of burning refuse.

Then, the sounds reached her.

14 Dawn in the Wasteland – The Hundred Project and Infection

Screams. Agonized, unrelenting. They wove through the darkness, mingling with inhuman growls. She froze, instincts urging her to retreat, but she had come too far.

Shadows shifted. Mutated figures—once human, now twisted by the virus that had ravaged their genetic code—snarled, igniting memories she had fought to bury. The Outer World was alive with horrors, and she was walking straight into its maw.

Within each host, the initial infection coursed through their veins like liquid fire, an intoxicating euphoria that made them feel invincible. Their senses sharpened, their strength surged, and their energy felt boundless—but the bliss was fleeting. The virus demanded sustenance; a relentless hunger satiated only by absorbing fresh, untainted DNA from the uninfected. Without it, the host decayed, their body twisting into grotesque aberrations, their mind unraveling into primal madness. The infection was a cruel trick—promising power before plunging its victims into an irreversible abyss.

Thirty-five blocks west and seventeen blocks south, past the skeletal remains of a lost city, Dawn approached the condemned building where she hoped to find answers. The structure loomed, its once-pristine façade now a battered relic, windows shattered, steel bones exposed. This was the birthplace of the horror that now plagued the world—the secret laboratories where the Twenty Project first began. Unbeknownst to her, it was also where the chaos of the Hundred Project had started, an experiment spawned from the Professor's fractured notes and Dawn's own DNA.

Steeling herself, she stepped inside, her boots echoing through the cavernous ruin. Dust swirled in the cold air. Her navigator, a voice crackling through her earpiece, broke the silence.

"Multiple heat signatures detected. You are not alone."

She tensed, eyes scanning the encroaching darkness. Shadows slithered through the wreckage, unnatural and erratic. A presence surrounded her—multiple presences. The navigator's urgent voice pressed in her ear, urging her to leave, but it was already too late.

The mutants surged from the shadows, their guttural snarls echoing off the decaying walls. Each step sent dust and debris cascading from the fractured ceiling, caught in the dim, flickering light.

Adrenaline flooded Dawn's veins, sharpening her senses. Training kicked in as she assessed the immediate threats: three mutants directly ahead, two flanking from the sides. Her mind raced, calculating distances, angles, potential escape routes.

"Navigator!" she barked, her voice cutting through the cacophony. "I need an out—now!"

"Stairwell to your left!" the navigator's voice crackled in her ear.

Dawn didn't hesitate. She pivoted, slamming her shoulder into the crumbling wall as she sprinted. The first mutant lunged, claws scraping the spot where she'd just been.

The stairwell offered no sanctuary. Grotesque sounds echoed from above, signaling the mutants had anticipated her move. Dawn slid to a halt, her back against the cold, damp stone. The air was thick with the stench of decay, each breath a reminder of the horrors closing in. No time for finesse—only survival.

"They're coming from both ends! Can you reroute?" she snapped.

"Negative, Dawn! It's a gamble either way!"

She spotted a loose metal pipe jutting from the wall. With a swift motion, she yanked it free, the rusted metal groaning in protest. The pipe became an extension of her arm, a makeshift weapon against the encroaching darkness.

The first mutant descended, its twisted face contorted in a silent scream. Dawn sidestepped, lashing out with the pipe, connecting with the creature's jaw. Bone cracked, and the mutant staggered, buying her a precious moment.

"Two more incoming! Upper level!" The navigator's warning was almost drowned out by the mutants' snarls.

Dawn whirled, swinging the pipe again, deflecting a clawed hand inches from her face. She had to create an opening.

Spotting a pile of rubble, she hurled the metal pipe at it, hoping to cause a distraction. The impact sent debris tumbling, a cloud of dust obscuring the stairwell as the mutants paused, momentarily disoriented.

"This isn't working!" Dawn yelled, her breath coming in ragged bursts. "I need another way out!"

The navigator's voice was strained. "There's a maintenance tunnel—a crawl space behind the walls thirty feet ahead to your left, but it's narrow."

Thirty feet might as well have been a mile. But Dawn knew she had no other choice.

"Where is it? I don't see an opening!" Panic edged her voice.

"Look along the base of the wall—it might look like an air vent."

Success.

She dropped to her knees, fingers scraping along the wall until they found the vent. She tore it open and crawled into the tunnel as the mutants pursued, their grotesque limbs raking at the plaster. The tunnel walls were damp and claustrophobic. She moved as fast as she could, the sounds of her predators growing closer, her hands raw and bleeding. Every inch was a battle.

The mutants were too large to follow, and their frustration mounted, their screeches echoing behind her. Finally, there was a break—the tunnel opened into a wider chamber.

"Where to now?" Her voice broke, exhausted. She could hear the slithering sounds of the horde approaching from all sides.

"Elevators. End of the corridor. Unlikely to be operational, but you might access the shaft."

She didn't wait for confirmation. She checked her remaining ammunition, took a deep breath, and moved. Gunfire erupted as she fought her way toward the elevator, bullets ripping through decayed flesh, the creatures shrieking in unnatural agony. Every strike, every kick, every exertion drained her reserves, but she couldn't stop.

Finally, she reached the elevators, pried the doors open with all her strength, and peered into the abyss of the shaft.

Darkness. Silence.

Then—a guttural growl from below.

No choice.

Gripping the thick steel cable hanging in the void, she launched herself into the vertical tunnel, her muscles screaming as she pulled herself upward. Below, the creatures had no intention of letting her escape. Their weight tugged at the cable, vibrations shuddering up her arms. One was climbing.

No—many were climbing.

She had seconds.

With her free hand, she fumbled for her pistol and fired blindly downward. Muzzle flashes lit the shaft in stuttering bursts. Screeches rose from below as infected bodies plummeted into the black depths. But there were always more.

"Twelfth floor," the navigator reminded her. "There's a blocked stairwell that might lead outside."

With a final burst of strength, she reached a ledge and hauled herself onto solid ground. Every fiber of her body burned. Her fingers trembled as she holstered her weapon. Her breaths came in ragged gasps.

Then she felt it.

Warmth. Wetness. A dull ache blossoming across her shoulder. Dread pooling in her stomach, she reached back, fingers grazing the torn fabric of her suit. Then—skin. Torn. Bloodied. A bite.

She staggered, the world tilting. No. No, not this.

Her vision swam as she fell to her knees, her body betraying her. "Navigator," she rasped, blinking against the encroaching darkness. "Navigator, come in... I need assistance..."

Static. Then—a voice. Familiar. Steady.

"Dawn, we've had you under observation. I got you."

Her heavy eyelids lifted just enough to see a figure approaching. The last thing she saw before oblivion took her was Matthew's face, his expression caught between relief and something else.

Then—darkness.

When she awakened, she was no longer in the ruins. A rhythmic hum filled the space around her. A helicopter. A transport. Overhead, the whirling blades cast shifting shadows. And beside her—Matthew. Watching. Waiting. Smiling.

She had survived.

But for how long?

15 ABDUCTION – PARTLOW'S LEGACY AND A NEW ASSIGNMENT

Six Weeks Later

Dawn's eyes fluttered open, her body attuned to the rhythm of the morning before the shrill chime of the alarm could disrupt the silence. The room was steeped in darkness, save for the soft glow of the city's artificial light filtering through the slanted blinds. She exhaled slowly, her breath merging with the stillness hanging in the air.

Sliding out of bed, she padded silently to the bathroom, where the hiss of the shower filled the space. Warm streams cascaded over her taut muscles, soothing yet relentless, as if trying to cleanse the stain of what she had done. She stood motionless beneath the downpour, her mind spiraling toward the inevitable conclusion of her recklessness.

They were coming. There was no question. The moment loomed, an unshakable force, ready to descend upon her with the full weight of consequence.

Last night, she killed a man. Not swiftly. Not cleanly. It had been gruesome—an act of violence painted in chaos. Her hands careless, her mind brazen, leaving behind evidence even the most incompetent investigator could trace. There was no undoing it.

The hunt had begun.

***

Forty-Eight Hours Earlier

The rhythmic pounding of her feet against the treadmill mimicked her racing thoughts. Sweat slicked her body, her breath measured yet fierce as she pushed through the final minutes of her morning workout. When the timer hit zero, she wiped her brow, stepped off the machine, and strode toward the shower, the routine ingrained in her.

Minutes later, wrapped in a towel, she saw the blinking notification on her tablet. A single message—encrypted, unmistakable. Her stomach clenched.

The Professor.

With a reluctant sigh, she tapped the screen, watching as the display flickered, then went black. The silence stretched before the screen lit again with a series of news segments.

Grainy images of missing persons, crime scenes, and anxious newscasters filled the display. Then, the Professor's unmistakable voice cut through the static.

"I'm sure you've seen and heard about the series of murders and abductions of women within Secure City 24. There was initially a media blackout, but when the authorities failed to secure a suspect or gain leads, they had no choice but to alert the public. However, I have some insight into what's happening."

Dawn folded her arms, her expression unreadable. "And since when did the affairs of individual cities become of interest to you? So what if a Secure City becomes a little less secure?" Her voice dripped with amusement. "The people need a reality check, a wake-up call."

The Professor's voice did not waver. "Under normal circumstances, I might agree with you. But this is different. I believe the Abductor may be of interest to us. I think we're dealing with a copycat."

Dawn arched a brow. "A copycat of what?"

"A case I worked on years ago," he continued. "One of the Agency's own went rogue—an agent by the name of Partlow. He spent nearly eight years committing a series of murders that we struggled to connect. His methods seemed erratic; his victims, random. But in time, we came to understand the philosophy behind his madness. He called it 'Order within Chaos.'"

He let those words sink in before continuing.

"We might never have caught him if not for his ego. He grew restless, craving recognition. That's when he began leaving notes, demanding the media blackout covering his crimes be lifted. He wanted an audience, so I gave him one. I made it personal, turned his vanity against him, and forced a mistake."

Dawn tilted her head, considering. "And when you caught him?"

"He laughed at us, mocked us, swore he'd never surrender his secrets. At first, we thought he only targeted women. We were wrong. He took men, the elderly, even children. He wasn't just a murderer—he was a trafficker. And the worst part?" The Professor's voice darkened. "His victims were sent to the Outer World. Many may still be alive, living as sex slaves... or worse."

A quiet tension filled the space. Dawn exhaled, her fingers tightening around the edge of the table. "And the secret he refused to spill?"

"He had a holding cell somewhere in the Outer World," the Professor said grimly. "We suspected he had accomplices—or at least, hoped he did. Before we could break him, he told us he had over twenty-five people locked away, among them the son of Ryne Lawson, Secure City 24's wealthiest citizen."

The Professor's voice dipped lower. "And then he clamped his mouth shut. No matter what we did, he wouldn't break."

We exhausted every method, both within the law and far beyond it. We started with civility, trying to coax him with reason. When that failed, we descended into the primal—resorting to violence, agony, unspeakable tortures meant to fracture his mind. But he never broke. Instead, he plunged deeper into madness, beyond pain or persuasion.

"Yet Ryne Lawson never gave up hope," the Professor intoned, his voice steady and deliberate. He was an orator, his cadence calculated, every word a measured strike against silence. "She believed, against all odds, that one day he would speak, that the families of the victims might finally have closure and reclaim the remains of their lost loved ones. Her resources seemed limitless, and with them, she ensured Agent Partlow was spared the death penalty. But in the end, his fate may have been worse—confinement in a special detention facility in the Outer World, a place where the line between prisoner and captor is indistinguishable; an asylum where the lunatics truly run the institution."

Dawn leaned forward, her gaze sharp and probing. "So you think Partlow is the key?" she asked, her voice betraying neither belief nor skepticism—just a demand for clarity.

The Professor tilted his head, amusement flickering in his eyes. "If not the key itself, then at least he understands how to unlock the door."

The plan that followed was laid out in that same infuriatingly composed manner, as if the Professor were mapping out an errand rather than a suicide mission. Nothing was ever easy, and this plan was as deranged as the man it revolved around.

Dawn was assigned to eliminate a government witness—an ex-judge preparing to testify against deeply entrenched corruption in the legal system. The assignment sat uneasily with her.

"But isn't that what we want?" she challenged. "Aren't we fighting the bad guys?"

The Professor smiled, idly tapping his fingers against the desk. "It's about balance, my dear. The world isn't broken; it's designed this way."

Dawn's stomach twisted. "You mean corrupted."

"No." His eyes gleamed with something colder than amusement. "I mean efficient."

He leaned forward, his voice smooth as glass. "Tell me—what is a machine without gears? What is a kingdom without a king?"

"A place where people are free," she shot back.

He chuckled, low and knowing. "No, my dear. A place without purpose. There will always be corruption. As long as an economic hierarchy exists, it is unavoidable. But corruption also serves our needs. It provides intelligence, weapons, safe passage, and leverage. It grants us favors, allows us to operate in the shadows where true power lies."

He paused, letting the weight of his words settle before delivering the final blow. "It is the lesser of two evils. And in our world, one cannot break the code without consequence. If we allow weakness, if we allow one defection, our power crumbles. True power is not measured in wealth but in reverence. And reverence, my dear, is merely fear in elegant disguise."

Dawn gave a half-hearted chuckle, laced with something between defiance and resignation. "I am no slave to life, nor do I fear death. But you have my respect, Professor."

The assassination was carried out with precision, but predictably, it was never meant to end with Dawn walking free. She was arrested, denied a trial—just another pawn in the Professor's grand game. And so she found herself in the same facility as Partlow, a prisoner in a world without reason, where insanity ruled and logic had long been abandoned at the gates.

Her mission? Seven days to find Partlow, extract the information he held, and eliminate him.

And then?

Escape.

Simple.

Except nothing was ever simple.

Dawn had her doubts. "If you did everything possible to make him talk and failed, what makes you think I'll have a better outcome?"

The Professor leaned forward, his expression almost indulgent. "Ah, my dear," he mused, "we tried everything masculine, everything forceful and brutal. But Partlow is a creature of depravity, driven by primal urges—sex and violence are his currencies, pain a perverse pleasure. To break him, you must exploit his sickness, tease him, taunt him, frustrate him beyond control. You have the key to his secrets."

Dawn smirked, shaking her head with a quiet laugh. "Men are like spoiled children."

The Professor simply smiled. "Indeed."

16 Assassin – Mission Conditions and Emotional Entanglements

The city lay in an eerie hush, a sprawling steel labyrinth bathed in the flickering glow of neon and the distant hum of electric patrol cruisers slicing through empty streets. Their high-pitched wails echoed off the towering structures, the only sounds breaking the suffocating silence of Secure City's enforced curfew. Amid the concrete and cold artificial light, a lone figure moved like a phantom, her silhouette flickering in and out of existence as she navigated the web of shadows cast by the city's relentless surveillance.

She counted heartbeats, syncing her movements to the rhythmic sweep of panning security cameras, calculating the precise interval between each patrol pass. With the precision of a seasoned predator, she darted across open spaces, pressing herself into the recesses of alleyways and doorframes, never lingering too long. Her goal was clear—a hotel on the outskirts of the district, its sixth-floor suite sheltering a man whose time had come.

The target's protection detail was stationed in the adjoining room, three trained officers standing between her and the completion of her mission. But walls were merely obstacles, and obstacles existed to be overcome. She slipped into the alley behind the hotel, her gaze tracing the skeletal fire escape zigzagging up the adjacent building. The ascent was swift, her boots soundless against the iron rungs as she scaled the structure with an efficiency honed by years of necessity. From the rooftop, she moved with feline agility, leaping across the chasm separating the buildings and landing in a crouch on the hotel's roof. The access hatch was her way in. Within moments, she was inside, descending into the stairwell unseen, unheard.

The hallway was dimly lit, the monotonous hum of cheap fluorescent bulbs barely masking the distant murmur of voices from within the rooms. She strode forward, shedding the cloak of the night for a different deception. With a practiced hand, she adjusted the neckline of her attire, ensuring that when the peephole was checked, all that would be visible were provocative curves.

Room 624 housed security. Room 622 held the prize. She knocked lightly on 624, shifting her body to obscure the peephole's view of anything beyond her lips and cleavage. When the door cracked open, she purred in a breathy, exaggerated accent.

"Sorry to disturb you this late, sir," she cooed, her voice honeyed with feigned nervousness. "I'm the room-service supervisor. One of our housekeeping staff misplaced a master key. Do you mind if I—"

The door swung open before she could finish. The unsuspecting officer turned, calling to his partner.

"Come take a look at this."

She stepped inside, her gaze sweeping the room with a predator's eye. One officer stood close, relaxed and oblivious. Another rose from one of the twin beds, his expression shifting from irritation to intrigue as he took in the unexpected visitor. Her mind registered every detail. Two bodies accounted for. One more unaccounted for, likely in the adjoining room with the target.

A plan crystallized, and she struck.

With a lightning-fast motion, her left leg shot back, the heel of her boot driving into the groin of the officer behind her. A strangled gasp escaped his lips as agony took hold, his body folding. In the same breath, she twisted, her hands snapping to his head—one gripping his chin, the other clenching his scalp. A sharp, decisive jerk, and his body went slack, collapsing.

The second officer barely had time to process the brutal efficiency before his fallen comrade was hurled into him, their tangled bodies toppling to the ground. She wasted no time, straddling them and raining down a barrage of precise, merciless strikes. Her fists and elbows became instruments of destruction, each impact drawing a fresh splatter of blood until the remaining officer's struggles ceased.

Silence reclaimed the room.

She rose, breath measured, ears tuned to the sounds beyond the adjoining door. The momentary stillness broke with a shuffle of movement. A shadow darkened the sliver of light beneath the door as it creaked open.

The third officer stepped into view, his sidearm leading the way. His mouth parted, perhaps to call out—but she was already upon him.

Her hands found the gun, twisting it from his grip as she yanked him off balance. His disarmed weapon became her own, and she wielded it without hesitation. The butt of the firearm cracked against the side of his skull, sending him reeling. Before he could recover, a forearm strike crashed into his neck, crushing his windpipe and dropping him to the floor.

The only sound remaining was the frantic, uneven breathing of the target—a man whose power and influence had afforded him protection, until now.

Judge Lemont Johnson stood frozen in horror, his gaze darting between the bodies littering the floor and the woman who had dispatched them with frightening ease. A dark stain spread across the front of his tailored slacks, the acrid scent of urine tainting the air.

She stepped forward, each movement deliberate, each heartbeat dragging his fate closer to its inevitable conclusion.

His final breath trembled past his lips as her shadow swallowed him whole.

17 GAMES OF THE COMPOUND

The moment Dawn's wrists were bound, her fate was sealed. There was no trial, no deliberation—just the swift and brutal judgment of Secure City's enforcers. She was ripped from the sterile, overregulated utopia and cast beyond its towering walls, into the untamed abyss of the Outer World. Here, laws were whispers in the wind, drowned out by the howling chaos of those who had long since abandoned civility. Yet even the lawless imposed order when it suited them. For the worst of the worst, there was a facility—a prison in name, though in truth, the entire Outer World was a prison of its own.

The facility loomed like a malignant tumor on the landscape, a grotesque monolith of stone, iron, and decay. Its massive, multi-tiered structure pulsed with the echoes of the damned—shouts, screams, and the occasional sob of the newly broken. This was where Dawn had been delivered, thrust into the hands of those who ran the place, unofficial wardens selected not for their discipline but their connections. The guards weren't officers of the law but a makeshift militia—a blend of gang enforcers, warlords' right hands, and mob muscle, each faction kept in check by a fragile, bloodstained truce inspired by perks dangled before each boss by the elites like lambs before slaughter. It was a system designed for failure, a keg of gunpowder trembling on the brink of detonation.

And Dawn? She could be the spark to set it alight.

On the surface, the facility was exactly what she expected—gray walls stained with sweat and despair, sour meals served on rusting trays, a lingering scent of antiseptic and humiliation. The guards barked orders more out of habit than authority, and the inmates shuffled like ghosts through routines designed to erase identity.

But Dawn wasn't here by mistake.

Her incarceration had been orchestrated—an intricate deception executed with surgical precision. The Professor's plan: seven days to find Charles Partlow, extract the truth, and eliminate him. But what no one told her was that this prison held far more than secrets—it was a theater of the grotesque, and beneath its surface lay a world as polished as it was perverse.

The upper tiers were misery and mediocrity. But the deeper Dawn descended—physically, politically—the more refined the architecture became. Monitors tracked inmates by the pulse, not the footstep. Cells transformed from cages into chambers. Eventually, the walls turned to brushed steel, glowing with biometric sensors and soft, ambient light.

They called it the Compound.

An underground society for the condemned, run not by wardens but by capital. This place wasn't designed to rehabilitate. It was designed to entertain.

From high above the facility's true infrastructure, international elites logged in through encrypted networks, watching everything from gladiator death matches to twisted sex rituals, placing bets and making requests with the ease of ordering takeout. For the right price, they could select an inmate for the evening—whether for pleasure, pain, or death.

And the mutants—twisted remnants of the 100 Project—were the star attractions. Some barely clung to humanity, while others had learned to restrain their transformation, balancing on a razor's edge between beast and man. Their battles with inmates were framed as sport, but the carnage was real.

Survival here wasn't just about strength, but performance, allegiances, submission, and resistance.

Dawn clocked it immediately.

The "privileges" offered weren't charity, but currency: trustees who policed the weak; artistic outlets as distractions; better meals as bribes; special assignments for those who proved useful beyond the walls. And those who were favored, chosen by clients?

They became Service Shadows—inmates granted momentary freedom to serve in the outside world, returning only when broken or bled dry.

Dawn's arrival rippled through the prison like a shockwave, news spreading with unnatural speed. She was processed with brutal efficiency—stripped, searched, and forced into a coarse uniform that did little to deter the leering eyes that fell upon her. There were no separate wings for men and women, just a mass of predators and prey. As she was led through corridors, inmates jeered and rattled bars. Guards made lewd remarks, suggesting her stay could be "pleasant" if she made the "right friends."

Dawn walked with measured steps, deliberately falling several paces behind the two corrections officers as she made a mental map of the surroundings and the twists of the labyrinthine corridors. Her eyes scanned everything, absorbing the grim realities of the Compound.

As she rounded a corner, she paused, an unspoken tension seizing the space ahead.

Near a reinforced steel door, an inmate knelt on the floor, her head bowed, face hidden, as she worked behind the utility belt of a burly guard who leaned against the wall, his eyes half-closed in bored indulgence. Another guard stood a few feet away, arms crossed, watching the scene with a passive gaze.

The kneeling inmate finished, rising slowly and smoothing down her stained jumpsuit. She avoided eye contact as she shuffled past Dawn, clutching something small in her hand—perhaps a stolen piece of candy or a momentary reprieve from a harder fate.

The watching guard pushed off the wall, stretching languidly. He met Dawn's gaze and offered a brief, humorless smirk. "Privates earn perks," he said, the words devoid of judgment or surprise.

The guard who had been serviced adjusted his belt. "Moving along, fish?" he grunted at Dawn, his voice gruff but carrying an undertone of expectation—a silent invitation to understand the transaction she had just witnessed.

Dawn said nothing, her expression unreadable. She continued down the hallway, leaving the casual exchange behind. The incident was not hidden; it was simply part of the scenery, understood and accepted by those who navigated this world.

Dawn was led to the infirmary for a brief physical, a formality performed half-heartedly to appease investors and limit potential outbreaks of sexually transmitted diseases. They drew blood and swabbed her nose, mouth, vagina, and anus before continuing toward her final destination.

One guard stopped abruptly, sniffing the air. "You smell that? She needs a shower." She was forced into a small, bare room reeking of mildew.

His partner sniffed the air, then leaned in toward Dawn, a grin splitting his face. "Yeah... I think this bitch needs a shower."

Without warning, rough hands clamped down on her arms, forcing her down a poorly lit corridor, away from the mass of prisoners. The walls were closer here, the light flickering in sickly bursts from failing fixtures above. They turned sharply into a small concrete room—cold, damp, and reeking of mildew.

"Strip down, fish."

One of the guards held a hose, its nozzle aimed at her with casual cruelty. The moment she hesitated, the icy blast struck her, drenching her in a wave of freezing water. Her body reacted instinctively, muscles seizing as the chill tore through her. Her skin prickled, nipples hardening under the assault—a detail not missed by the guards.

"Damn," one muttered, licking his lips. "Look at the body on this one. I'm first this time."

"Bullshit." His partner scoffed, shifting. "All you ever want is head, and that takes too damn long. I'm going first. I'll hit that tight little—"

Dawn had stopped listening.

She stood still, water streaming from her hair, pooling at her feet. Her gaze fixed on the guard before her, cold and unwavering. She sized him up, noting the way his stance favored his left leg, the twitch in his fingers. Short. Weak. A pathetic excuse for a man whose sense of power stemmed from a uniform that meant nothing in a world already forsaken.

In her mind, she was already stripping him—not in the way he imagined, but for utility. His boots? Probably her size. His boxers? She could use those. Maybe even his partner's tank top. His own? Not a chance. That would be too soaked in the blood he was about to spill.

A slow, deliberate smirk curved Dawn's lips as she took a step forward, unfazed by her nakedness. If they thought she was another helpless lamb tossed to slaughter, they were dead wrong.

And soon, they would know it.

The dim overhead lights buzzed softly, casting long shadows across the prison corridor's cold concrete walls. The air reeked of sweat, rust, and the faint metallic tang of old blood. The silence was broken only by the steady rhythm of approaching boots, deliberate and heavy, like a countdown.

A burly guard strode forward, tightening his grip on his security baton. His gaze was sharp, predatory, zeroing in on the lone figure standing defiantly in the corridor's center.

"Dawn," he said, his voice smugly confident. "We can do this the easy way, or the hard way."

Dawn's rigid posture softened into something sinuous, laced with dark amusement. A slow, sultry smile curled her lips as if a different persona had slipped into place.

"You think I'm new to this?" she purred, her voice a velvet caress wrapped around steel. "I know how the game works. I'm all about easy, baby. The only thing I want hard is you. Now, put that nightstick away. I won't hurt you."

Fluidly, she sank into a slow squat, positioning herself in front of the guard's crotch. Her hands, light as feathers, skimmed up his thighs in a teasing glide, inching toward his groin with tantalizing patience. Her gaze flickered up through thick lashes, coy yet inviting.

"You wanna fuck me in my ass?" Her voice dipped lower, honeyed and submissive, weaving a spell of seduction. "I'm ready, but why don't you let me get you right first? Can you handle some deepthroat?"

She flicked her tongue upward in a serpentine motion. The guard, caught in the intoxicating snare of desire and arrogance, mirrored her, sticking out his tongue like a fool. In his eagerness, his grip loosened, and the baton clattered to the floor. His belt unfastened, his pants dropped, and for a moment, the air thickened with unspoken anticipation.

Then, in a sudden burst, Dawn sprang upward, the crown of her skull cracking against the guard's chin with bone-rattling force. His mouth snapped shut, and the wet, grotesque squelch of severed flesh filled the air as he bit through his own tongue. His head snapped back, exposing his throat.

Dawn didn't hesitate. Her fingers latched onto the vulnerable flesh with unrelenting precision as she twisted, wrenching with vicious force. A sickening rip echoed through the corridor as his throat tore free, arterial spray painting a crimson arc across the walls.

Before his body registered death, she followed through with a ruthless back kick, her heel slamming into his sternum like a sledgehammer. The brutal impact shattered bone, forcing a gasp from his ruined throat. He wavered, knees buckling as he tumbled backward, his lowered pants tangling around his legs. The unforgiving concrete rushed up, and his skull cracked against the floor with a sickening thud. He convulsed, desperate for oxygen, the gurgling choke of his own blood drowning him.

The wet, grotesque sound slithered through the air, drawing attention. Dawn turned her head, her eyes catching the shifting shadow stretching across the floor—another figure approaching. She bent down, fingers curling around the fallen nightstick, her stance still, breath measured.

The second guard stepped into view, his face twisting in confusion at his partner's sprawled body.

With a calculated flick of her wrist, she launched the baton. The timing was impeccable. The guard barely registered movement before the weapon cracked against his skull. His head snapped sideways, the force throwing him off balance as Dawn surged forward. Like a predator, she closed the distance in a blink, her body crashing into his legs. He toppled, his back slamming into the ground, and before he could recover, Dawn was on him.

Straddling his chest, she rained down blows with unrelenting fury, her elbows cutting through the air like daggers. Each strike landed with a sickening impact, bone crunching. The side of his head caved; his limbs twitched, spasmed, then fell still.

Dawn exhaled, slow and steady, rolling her shoulders as she straightened. The silence returned, thick and suffocating, broken only by the faint, rhythmic drip of blood pooling onto the floor. She retrieved the fallen baton, her fingers tightening around the handle. There would be more coming. There always were.

But she was ready.

Her defiance was noted. Not punished—not immediately. Instead, the guards dragged her to her new confines.

The air in the cell was a pungent mix of disinfectant and stale sweat. Dressed in a simple tank top, boxers, and a pair of well-worn boots— spoils of her conquest and a visual note stating, "Don't fuck with me"—she sat on the metal-framed bunk, her back straight, her expression unreadable. The dim light from the corridor filtered through the iron bars, casting long, jagged shadows across the gray concrete walls. She knew they would come for her; it was only a matter of time.

She didn't have to wait long.

The light beyond the bars dimmed as a group of figures loomed in the corridor, their broad silhouettes exuding dominance. The leader stepped forward, a hulking woman with a jawline chiseled from stone and arms thick with muscle. Her grin was predatory, flashing white teeth as she took in Dawn's form.

"Looking good, Ma," the woman rumbled, her voice dripping with possessiveness. "I think you're my new cow. I'mma call you Bambi."

Beside her, a petite, pale-skinned girl—nervous and eager to please— flinched, her wide eyes darting between Dawn and her leader. "But... but I'm your Bambi!" she stammered. "She's not even in uniform."

"Nah, but what she got on is kinda sexy. I think that's my new Bambi," the towering woman said dismissively. "Get up off that bunk and come with me to your new home, bitch." She motioned for the smaller woman to step inside the cell as if swapping out possessions.

Dawn moved slowly, deliberately, rising from her bunk with a calculated grace that spoke of experience. She tilted her head from side to side, vertebrae popping, then rolled her shoulders back, stretching out the tension.

She watched the leader with cold amusement.

"My name's not Bambi," she said, her voice soft but laced with the promise of violence. "And I ain't nobody's bitch."

The leader chuckled, her bulk filling the doorway. "Oh, we got one. You think you're tough, huh?"

Dawn took a slow step forward, letting the light catch the edge of her smirk. "I don't think," she murmured. "I know."

A flicker of uncertainty crossed the leader's face—brief, but Dawn saw it, and she would use it.

She gestured subtly for the pale girl to step aside, her sharp gaze raking over the group just beyond the cell's entrance. A mental checklist formed—who was the biggest threat, who would hesitate, who would run.

The leader, her massive frame filling the doorway, cracked her knuckles. Her breathing quickened, a ragged inhale followed by a sudden, disturbing shift. Her already imposing body seemed to expand, muscles contorting and bulging as if something unnatural lurked beneath her skin. Her facial features hardened, jawline thickening, brow ridge growing more pronounced.

"She's a mutant," Dawn realized, her heartbeat slowing rather than quickening. "Could this be one of the 100 Projects?"

Behind her, the pale girl shrank into the corner of the cell, trembling violently as though sensing the impending explosion of violence.

Then, the alarm blared.

"Lockdown! Everyone back to your cells, this is a lockdown!" The voice over the PA system rang out with sharp authority, bouncing off the cold walls.

A flicker of irritation crossed the mutant's beastly face, but she obeyed, stepping back just beyond the cell's threshold.

A potential clash averted, the real Bambi—a fragile being—slipped Dawn a look that said help me.

With a snap of her fingers, the small pale girl scrambled to her side, frail fingers grasping the mutant's waistband like a child clinging to a parent.

"This ain't over, fish," the mutant growled, her voice deeper, more guttural, promising future violence.

As the heavy metal doors slid shut, locking the prisoners in for the night, Dawn leaned back against the cold wall, exhaling slowly. Two hours into the first day, and she had already made an enemy. She smirked to herself, the ceiling a blank slate for her thoughts.

"This is going to be interesting…" she murmured.

The PA system crackled to life again. "Two of our guards were killed today, and this goes out to whoever did this… You won't be leaving here alive!"

Dawn closed her eyes, letting the weight of her mission settle over her. She had six days left. Six days to find Partlow. Six days to get him to talk. Six days to escape.

The problem was she still had no idea how.

18 THE QUEEN OF BLOOD

Dawn learned her name in whispers during the aftermath: Big Les. A towering mutant woman with skin like leather and fists like mallets. A product of one of the earliest Virus Series—no longer fully human. Not fully anything. She reigned over the underground Death Circuit, a seasonal gladiatorial contest she'd ruled undefeated across seventeen sanctioned bouts—and countless unsanctioned ones.

But Les didn't just kill. She collected.

Her favorite trophy was a broken girl she called Bambi.

A wraith in lace. Pale, trembling. Always by Les's side. Scarred in places that hadn't healed right. Fresh bruises. A makeshift collar around her throat, more symbolic than practical—everyone knew Bambi was Les's to do with as she pleased.

Further down the tier, behind another set of locked bars, Big Les lay awake, her body still thrumming with unused aggression. She turned her head slightly, eyes glinting in the dimness.

"Bambi," she said, her voice deceptively soft, "you wanna come over here tonight?"

The smaller girl shook her head vigorously, her refusal almost too quiet to hear.

The mutant's lips curled in a cruel smile. "Bitch, this ain't no democracy. I wasn't asking. Get your narrow ass in bed with me."

The night pressed on, thick and oppressive, filled with the sounds of shifting bodies, whispered threats, and the ever-present hum of desperation.

Morning arrived too soon, dispelling the last vestiges of sleep as the prison stirred. Steel doors clanged through the cellblock, punctuated by the rhythmic thud of marching boots. Inmates emerged groggily from restless sleep, stretching sore limbs in preparation for another day in confinement.

But one prisoner was already awake.

Dawn sat cross-legged in the middle of her cell, her breath measured and steady. Beads of sweat cooled on her skin, the result of a grueling conditioning regimen she had just completed. Eyes closed, mind sharpened, she meditated, awaiting the inevitable storm.

A commotion shattered the morning's fragile peace. Guards thundered past her cell, their urgency palpable. Other inmates pressed against the bars, craning their necks, their voices a cacophony of speculation. Through the frenzy, a phrase broke through—an urgent call over a guard's radio for a doctor from the infirmary.

Later, Dawn learned the emergency involved a petite inmate known as Bambi, who had been rushed to the prison hospital after another unexplained medical episode. A hushed conversation among the guards suggested this wasn't the first time Bambi had been found in distress, but this time, it was far worse.

A guard appeared at Dawn's cell, his expression unreadable. "You're coming with me," he said, motioning for her to follow.

Dawn was led through a maze of hallways to the infirmary, where the sharp scent of antiseptic burned her nostrils. Nearing Bambi's room, she caught snippets of a conversation between two doctors.

"I don't think she's going to make it this time," one murmured gravely.

"This time?" the other asked, voice laced with concern.

"She's been in here before, but this… this is different. It's as if something is siphoning the life out of her. Last time, we kept her under observation, gave her fluids, increased her nutritional intake, and she bounced back. We initially thought anemia, but her bloodwork came back clean. We even checked for HIV and other infections—nothing. The only anomaly was some strange antibodies found in her vaginal fluids. We're still waiting on further tests, but whatever this is, it's not contagious. Small mercy, I suppose."

Dawn entered the sterile room, her gaze falling upon Bambi's frail form. The girl lay motionless, her skin pale, eyes sunken with exhaustion. Her frailty was haunting. A guard stepped aside, leaning in to whisper, "She asked to see you."

Dawn moved closer, her voice soft. "Hey, lil' bit. I'm here. You wanted to see me?"

Bambi's lips trembled as she forced out weak, ragged words. "She's killing me. She'll kill you too… I'd rather die than go back to that cell with her."

Her breath came in sharp, painful gasps. "Every time she goes down on me, I get weaker. Last night, I begged her to stop. It was like she was sucking the life out of me." Her voice was brittle, lips cracked, eyes sunken.

Dawn gently rubbed Bambi's forehead. "Lil' bit, how… how did things get this bad? Before Les…"

Bambi's eyes fluttered open, meeting Dawn's gaze. A tear tracked down her cheek. "Before Les claimed her, she was a trustee, passed around between guards and med techs in exchange for painkillers and protection."

Her voice was barely a whisper, thick with shame and pain. "To survive the bottom. It's... it's how some of us get by. If you can't fight, you... you find another way. The guards... they like trustees they can trust. And the med techs... they have things people need." She shuddered. "But Les... she's different. She takes everything."

Dawn understood: Les wasn't just a predator—she was using Bambi to fuel her mutation. Something deeper was being protected here. A dark certainty settled in her gut. This confirmed what she had begun to suspect.

"She's one of the 100 Project," Dawn thought grimly, gently rubbing Bambi's forehead in silent consolation.

Dawn's jaw tightened. It wasn't just random acts of violence, but a system. Even a slightly privileged status like "trustee" was just another layer of vulnerability, another commodity in the prison's brutal economy.

19 LEVEL ONE: THE TEST

Leaving the infirmary, she was escorted to the chow hall. The scent of overcooked food and stale air made her stomach turn, but she took her tray and found a secluded table. The quiet was short-lived. A shadow loomed behind her, and a familiar, venomous voice cut through the ambient noise.

"You and me got business to finish, bitch."

Dawn took a measured bite of her food, chewing slowly before responding. "I figured out what you are," she said calmly, barely glancing over her shoulder. "You and the other ninety-nine... you're abominations."

Deep, guttural breathing filled the space behind her. Dawn smirked slightly. "You'd probably have a better chance of surprising me with your transformation if it wasn't for all that damned breathing."

She moved swiftly. In one seamless motion, she leaned forward, then snapped her body backward, slamming the back of her skull into the mutant's midsection. The force sent the attacker reeling, gasping. Dawn capitalized on the moment, launching upward and striking her squarely in the throat.

"It's hard to do your little quick-change trick when you can't breathe," she taunted, before planting both feet into the mutant's sternum and sending her crashing over a table.

The chow hall erupted into chaos. Guards swarmed to prevent a full-scale riot as the mutant's crew bristled with tension, watching their leader crumble beneath Dawn's blows.

Her defiance did not go unnoticed. She was dragged into solitary confinement, but word of her actions spread like wildfire.

The very intrigued Partlow took an interest in her.

Dawn had been transferred to the special ward after dismantling Big Les. Killing two guards and confronting a champion earned her attention, not punishment.

"Quite the résumé," a voice in the shadows purred.

"Who are you?" Dawn asked.

"All in good time. There's no rush. Neither of us are going anywhere. I just needed to see for myself the woman who dropped Big Les. Your little display has everyone buzzing."

The picture became clearer as scenes clicked into place in her head; it was the season of the Death Circuit.

"With your skills, your stay here could be considerably nicer. You just have to know when and how to retract those claws. What a gifted, dangerous, and beautiful pussy you are." His voice flowed with intention.

"Pussy?" she snapped.

"As in cat—the way you move and strike without warning. An adjective of endearment; no disrespect intended."

"Yet still no introduction."

Now Dawn knew who—and why.

Partlow had been the facility's crown jewel. His depravity was part of the attraction. His violence, a curated experience. But beneath the smug charm and perversions lay something real—a vault of secrets about human-trafficking rings, disappeared agents, and black-market connections too sensitive for daylight. That's why the Professor needed him gone.

And it was why Dawn had to move quickly. This prison was not just a holding cell—it was a marketplace, a performance hall, a slaughterhouse. If she didn't kill Partlow soon, she risked becoming part of the product line.

Her performance was too clean, too effective. It brought a "recruiter"—not an oily executive, but someone who made it clear she was being watched and that they'd offered her "advancement." Her mission had collided with their recruitment program. She was a potential champion, someone who could make the house money.

But Dawn already had her target. Partlow was the rot. He played both sides—feeding the system its monsters while grooming prospects for off-site contracts. A handler. A pimp. A gatekeeper. And his power came not from muscle, but secrets.

The Professor needed those secrets silenced. Dawn wanted to understand them first.

And she would...

The next day, she was escorted to the top floor of the prison—an area that looked nothing like a traditional cell. The space was expansive, more akin to a lavish penthouse than a prison. Silk curtains divided sections of the room, a striking contrast to the cold metal and stone of the rest of the facility.

A man emerged from behind one of the curtains, draped in a silk kimono robe. He stood in the shadows, his face obscured.

"Welcome, Ms…?" His voice was smooth, almost hypnotic.

"Dawn," she replied evenly.

"Dawn," he repeated, savoring the name. "Fitting for a woman who has brightened my day."

"And how have I done that?" she asked, arching a brow.

He chuckled. "Two guards and Big Les. You have my attention. Big Les is one of my enforcers, managing newly acquired assets. She often finds me… promising prospects. I have very particular tastes. Not just anyone piques my interest, but you… you've surpassed all expectations."

Dawn feigned ignorance. "I still don't understand."

"All in time, my dear," he assured her. "How do you like your new surroundings?"

She took in the opulence. "My new surroundings?" she echoed.

"Wouldn't you like to stay here for a while?" he asked, unwavering. "It would relieve some pressure. Big Les needs to save face, and the guards? They won't take what you did to their comrades lightly."

She played coy, gathering intel. He let her linger—tempting her with safety, protection, comfort. But her mission never left her mind.

Dawn hesitated. As much as she wanted to refuse, his logic was sound.

"What makes this place so special?" she asked, narrowing her eyes. "Who are you? Some kind of super-criminal?"

He laughed, stepping into the light. Dawn was caught off guard—he was strikingly handsome.

This just got interesting.

***

He lived on the east wing—luxurious by prison standards. Silk robes, citrus water, imported teas, music piped through a hidden sound system. But it wasn't status—it was protection. Reserved for those who knew too much.

He had outside contacts. Contraband runners. Access to names, locations, an endless list of their most depraved secrets. It wasn't power that kept him alive, but leverage and fear. Everyone wanted something from him, but no one wanted to be the one to silence him.

Dawn played along, hoping to gain his trust, decoding his rhythms. But her mind never left Bambi.

The dim, flickering light cast long shadows along the cracked concrete walls. The scent of sweat and stale breath settled between them—an unspoken challenge. The faint hum of distant murmurs and the occasional clang of metal set the stage: a place where power was currency and fear a commodity.

"I'm not a super-criminal, just someone who knows how to capitalize on opportunities. I suggest you do the same," he said, his voice a low rumble. His gaze was piercing, a predator sizing up its next move. "As long as you're here with me, you're safe. And if you want to stay that way, you'd better prepare yourself."

Dawn smirked, her tone dripping with derision as she leaned back. "Prepare for what? You wanna fuck?" she scoffed, cocking an eyebrow. "If I didn't get with the big dyke, what makes you think I'm gonna get with you?"

His laughter slithered through the air, cold and sharp. "Sex is the least of your worries." He stepped closer, eyes glinting with something darker than hunger.

"My passion stems from something far more primal. What arouses me has little to do with pleasure… and everything to do with pain."

Dawn didn't flinch, a slow, knowing smirk curling her lips. "You like breaking things, don't you?" she murmured. "I do too. But I don't just break—I shatter."

The air between them tightened. He hesitated—just for a second, but that was all she needed.

"Well, Dawn, that all depends on you," he murmured, his voice like gravel scraping steel. "I know what I like and what I'm willing to tolerate. It's up to you to play the game and find out whether your stay here is pleasurable... or something else entirely."

Dawn rolled her shoulders back, exhaling sharply. "I don't really like games, but I'll play. And since we're in a playful mood, why don't you tell me who you are and why you hold so much power in here? What makes you so special?"

Silence. He halted, standing directly before her, their eyes locking like two titans readying for war. The energy in the room coiled tight, poised to snap. Dawn's lips curled into a knowing smirk.

"I know your type," she said, her voice steady, sharp as a blade. "You get off on hurting people. Seeing fear in their eyes makes your dick hard. You're a blood-and-pain freak who can't even get it up without violence." She took a single step closer. "You're a pathetic, weak, soft-dicked worm who hits women just to feel like a man."

The moment shattered. He lunged, seizing a fistful of her hair and yanking her forward until their noses nearly touched, the heat of his breath burning against her face, his grip vice-like.

"Bitch, I could kill you right now, and no one would question it," he snarled, his voice a venomous hiss. "I could chop you into countless little pieces and have you served as stew for tomorrow's meal. Do you even know who the fuck you're talking to?"

Dawn met his fury with an almost maddening calm. Slowly, seductively, she ran her tongue across her lips before biting down, drawing blood. A single ruby droplet trickled down her chin.

Partlow's confidence wavered, his grip hesitating as his eyes flicked to the crimson trail. Dawn saw the flicker of uncertainty and pressed forward.

"Wouldn't you like to put your cock in my mouth?" she whispered, voice a siren's call, dangerous and alluring. "Feel my blood drip down your balls?"

His breath hitched, confusion evident. "What the fuck are you doing?" he demanded, his voice an uneasy mix of arousal and suspicion.

Dawn's smirk deepened. "What do you wanna do?" she countered.

His grip tightened, yanking her closer, fingers digging into her scalp. "I wanna punch you in your fuckin' face."

Dawn inhaled sharply, closing her eyes as if savoring the moment. Then, in one fluid motion, she dropped to her knees. The sudden movement startled him, but he recovered quickly, tilting her head back with an iron grip. He pulled back his fist and delivered a crushing blow to the side of her face. Her body rocked from the impact, but she barely wavered.

She licked at the corner of her mouth, tasting copper. "You hit like a bitch," she muttered, voice steady despite the sting. "Are you sure that's hard enough to get your flaccid dick up?"

Irritated, he struck again, harder this time. Dawn crumpled to the ground but was yanked back up by her hair, her face pressed against his crotch.

"Is this hard enough for you, bitch?" he bellowed. "I'm gonna skull-fuck your face raw."

Dawn chuckled low, the sound vibrating against him. Slowly, she dragged her hands up his thighs, her fingers teasingly close to the growing heat beneath his robe. His breath grew ragged, anticipation lacing his movements as he parted the fabric.

But instead of the warmth of her mouth, a sharp, sudden pain jolted through him. Dawn's fingers clamped down on his testicle with a vice grip.

"Oh, shit," he groaned, a strange mixture of pain and pleasure in his voice.

Dawn knew she had him. Her fingers twisted, delivering a jolt of agony that made him shudder. She grinned, then unleashed a barrage of punches to his lower abdomen, sending him staggering backward. In an instant, she was on him, mounting his torso as he hit the cold ground.

For a moment, they lay motionless, the heat of battle simmering. Then, a wicked grin spread across Dawn's face. She repositioned herself, straddling his face with domineering force.

"Eat my ass, bitch," she commanded, grinding into him.

Partlow groaned, breath ragged, restraint shattered. As she rode his face, he reached beneath his robe, his excitement reaching a fever pitch. The crude, debasing act sent him spiraling over the edge, his body convulsing as he succumbed to his own depravity.

Dawn leaned forward, whispering against his ear as he gasped for breath beneath her. "Looks like I won this round."

She rose, her movements slow and deliberate, leaving Partlow sprawled on the cold floor, his body trembling, breath ragged. Dim light flickered through the bars, casting long shadows across the walls. As she turned, a flicker of movement outside caught her eye. Her spine straightened, muscles tensing. Beyond the bars, a dark silhouette shifted, the soft shuffle of retreating footsteps betraying a guard.

Dawn stepped forward, pressing her palm against the cool metal of the door; it gave way. Unlocked. Adrenaline surged, but before she could move, she saw the guard slip into the shadows. The invitation was clear, but the intention remained a mystery.

Turning back, she hesitated at the threshold, scanning for Partlow. The spot where he had lain was empty. Her pulse quickened, stance shifting defensively. Movement in her periphery stilled her. There, in the corner, nestled in a lavish, oversized bed that had no business being there, lay Partlow, relaxed, his breath even. The stark contrast between the bleak walls and the custom king-sized bed made her stomach twist. This was no ordinary incarceration.

Dawn exhaled slowly, peeling off her clothing before slipping beneath the sheets. Partlow stirred, gravitating toward her, his arms wrapping around her with a warmth that was both foreign and disarming. Without words, they settled into the night, fitting together like a puzzle. The quiet hum of their breathing filled the cell as they drifted into sleep, spooning beneath the weight of unspoken truths.

Morning arrived not with the sterile scent of prison, but with the unexpected aroma of freshly brewed coffee, coaxing Dawn from slumber. Partlow stood in the doorway, a steaming cup in his hand, his expression unreadable.

"I wasn't sure how you take it," he said, his voice softer than she had ever heard it. "Cream and sugar okay?"

A small smile played at her lips as she accepted the cup, the warmth seeping into her palms. She took a sip, savoring the moment, then extended her hand, fingers curling in invitation.

"Come talk to me," she murmured, her tone laced with something unspoken.

Partlow's smirk was slow, laced with mischief, as he set the cup aside. "I can think of better uses for our mouths," he said, voice suggestive as he climbed onto the bed, lips finding the curve of her breast before beginning a slow descent.

Dawn's fingers tangled in his hair, her grip tightening as she yanked his face away. "No, not right now," she insisted, voice firm. "I want to talk."

The shift was immediate. Partlow's expression darkened, his body stiffening with irritation. "Damn it!" he snapped, pushing himself up. "What is with this talk shit? Is this a fucking interrogation?" His voice rose, laced with frustration. "I'm trying to be nice to you! Why won't you let me?!"

Dawn acted swiftly, her palm colliding with his cheek in a sharp slap that echoed through the room. His breath hitched, his eyes flaring with shock and something deeper—something primal.

"Stop bitching and lay down," she commanded, her voice unwavering.

A tense silence settled between them, charged and volatile. Then, slowly, he relented, sinking back onto the bed. Dawn leaned in, pressing a kiss to his chest, her tongue tracing a path downward, teasing, promising. His body responded instantly, muscles taut, need evident.

And then—she pulled away.

Without a word, she pushed off the bed and strode toward the adjoining bathroom. "I need a shower," she threw over her shoulder.

"What the fuck?!" Partlow's outraged yell followed her, but she didn't turn back.

Being with Partlow had its advantages and provided her with privileges. She set off freely and unattended to the infirmary to check on Bambi.

20 THE RIPPLE EFFECT

She heard the thud before she saw it. Infirmary hall. A girl—couldn't have been more than eighteen—curled up as a trustee named Janko kicked her in the ribs. A routine show of dominance. The other inmates averted their eyes. No one moved. The guards didn't blink.

Dawn stepped between them without a word.

Janko laughed. "You want next, BITCH?"

She didn't respond. A sharp palm to his throat dropped him to the ground; a stomp to his leg shattered his kneecap.

The silence that followed was deafening. The girl gasped through broken sobs. Janko howled. The guards... still didn't move.

Dawn continued through the infirmary in search of Bambi. One of the inmates slipped her a ration fruit bar in appreciation and whispered that Bambi was no longer there. Prying eyes prevented more; the woman simply pointed downward and scurried away.

Dawn moved about the prison with the revelry of a superstar. Countless inmates acknowledged her with silent gestures, afraid of retribution, but it was clear she had sparked something among them.

ALLEGIANCES FORMED

Whispers spread like heat: "The new one's not afraid." "She dropped Janko like nothing." "She might be one of them."

Them, meaning Plant. Them, meaning dangerous. Them, meaning MUTANT.

She tried to lay low, focus on Partlow, observe Les, and keep her footing. But the prison had its own gravitational pull—and Dawn was becoming a center of mass.

The inmates began to shift—not just in awe, but in alignment.

A soft revolution ignited in the cracks of routine. Some—those long brutalized—started following her through the mess line. Others began resisting, quietly. One refused a guard's advance. Another stood shoulder to shoulder with Dawn in the shower corridor when Les passed by.

Not a word was spoken, but everyone felt it.

She was changing the gravity.

LOYALTY LINES

Another altercation erupted in the rec pit. Two inmates were baited into a fight for the guards' amusement—standard procedure. One of the weaker ones, Reyes, was losing badly until Dawn interfered, sending a metal plate spinning with a precise throw. The fight broke down fast, guards flooding in with tasers, but the outcome was clear:

Dawn had chosen a side.

The other fighters never looked at her the same again—not with fear, but with expectation.

By that evening, the prison had fractured.

Two sects emerged:

- The CPs (compound privileged) – inmates aligned with Les, the trustees, and the guards. Violent and opportunistic, loyal to no one but power.

- The Groundsliders – worthless worms to the CPs. The abused, the discarded, the forgotten. Those who saw Dawn as something more— not a savior, but a symbol.

WATCHING EYES

The hidden surveillance systems recorded everything. Live feeds went out to elite voyeurs, administrators, and handlers, all watching in silence.

Dawn's combat stats were flagged, her interactions with Partlow logged, and her face added to the roster.

She was being groomed for the Arena—not as cannon fodder, but as a contender.

Those whispers became a thunderous noise that clashed with the tranquility Partlow had established for himself.

A FRAGILE CODE

Inside the Compound, peace was maintained through fear and a fragile code of conduct. It was co-ed, dangerous, and brutally hierarchical. Dawn could feel the eyes on her. Mutants respected strength. Psychopaths respected fear. But the true monsters respected only one thing—utility.

The time was quickly approaching for Partlow to offer her a secondary proposal. One that was not necessarily a request, because it required he divulge the truth behind the Compound.

In the days that followed, their twisted game unfolded—a calculated dance of pursuit and denial. Dawn led, Partlow followed, their dynamic shifting with each touch, each stolen moment. She teased, tempted, and withheld, exploiting the depraved hunger she had uncovered beneath his violent tendencies.

One morning, over a breakfast more extravagant than prison life should allow, Partlow began to unravel. Dawn bit into a strawberry he had fed her, the juice sweet on her tongue.

"I grew these myself," he admitted, tone casual, but with a flicker of something else beneath it. "We have a green roof."

Dawn raised a brow, intrigued. "A prison full of criminals, and you're all gardeners?"

Partlow chuckled, his expression uncharacteristically light. "Hard to believe, right? Would you like to see it?"

"Yes," she answered, holding his gaze. The moment stretched between them, shifting.

21 LEVEL TWO: THE INVITATION

Partlow became her informant and her test, teasing the truth over meals grown in his personal greenhouse. This prison wasn't a facility; it was a marketplace.

Partlow lounged on his opulent bed, swirling amber liquid in his glass as he watched Dawn. He had revealed the prison's inner workings—that it was a marketplace for staged fights, sex acts, and experiments, with the lower tiers as fodder. He saw her potential, her defiance, and knew she was more than just cannon fodder.

"The lower tiers," Partlow said, swirling the drink, "are the raw material, the entertainment. But the truly useful... graduate."

Dawn raised an eyebrow. "Graduate to what?"

Partlow smirked. "Special assignments," he said, emphasizing the words with a subtle twist. "Sometimes... they leave. For a time."

He took a slow sip. "Clients outside have very specific needs. And we have a supply of... adaptable people who can play a role. They earn privileges, time outside."

He gestured around his opulent room. "This? This is nothing compared to what some of them get, provided they return and are... functional." He paused, eyes glinting. "They call them Service Shadows. Because they slip in and out of the real world without a trace. Until they don't."

The term hung heavy with implication. The exploitation extended beyond these walls, connecting the prison's depravity to the real world and its elite clientele.

The casual way they discussed lives being bought, sold, and staged for entertainment sent a chill down Dawn's spine. It wasn't about justice or rehabilitation; it was about product and profit.

"They've been running diagnostics," Partlow said, his voice casual but his eyes sharp. "Since your little 'incident' downstairs. The lab boys are buzzing."

Dawn narrowed her eyes. "Lab work? What for?"

"Curiosity, mostly," he shrugged—though she knew him well enough to see the lie. "You're not exactly standard issue, are you, Dawn?" He paused, leaning forward. "The lab work shows your genetic code and resistance to the mutation gene are unique. Your body... fights things off differently and heals unnaturally fast. The mutation gene that twists the others... it just bounces off you." He smirked. "Makes sense, I suppose. You took down one of the Hundred Project, after all. Maybe you're designed to handle them. Or maybe... you're something else entirely."

Dawn felt a familiar chill settle in her gut. Designed. The Professor's words echoed in her mind: I created you. This lab work wasn't just about understanding her resistance; it was confirming her suspicions about her unnatural nature.

"What does this mean?" she asked, her voice flat.

"It means," Partlow said, his smirk widening, "you're not going anywhere. Not just yet."

Dawn's combat stats were flagged. Her interactions with Partlow, logged. Her face added to the roster. She was being groomed for the Arena—not as cannon fodder, but as a contender.

He raised his glass in a silent toast. "Welcome to the next level, contender."

Fights were staged and streamed. Clients with deep wallets requested shows: death matches, sex acts, experiments in control. The prisoners below were fodder, their suffering commodified.

There were layers:

- The Ground Tier: traditional population; guards controlled by gangs; mutants enforced order—the code of violence.

- The Second Tier: medical experiments; mutants kept alive and stimulated for conditioning.

- The Third Tier: private selections; inmates trained, rewarded, and rented out for special assignments—both inside and outside the facility.

- The Compound: beneath the surface; a hyper-sanitized, high-tech arena reserved for blood sport, combat between altered beings and human warriors, streamed to a sick, paying audience.

Those who survived gained access to "trustee" status. With enough kills or cooperation, some were even given time outside to serve clients in the real world.

Dawn pondered this new revelation, piecing together her next move—and her reaction to Partlow. Could this be what the inmate meant by pointing down? Might Bambi be there? She had to find out. But how would she access it? Could she coerce Partlow into taking her? Or just ask him?

Later, under the warm spray of the shower, his lips ghosted over her neck, his breath hot against her skin. His hands were surprisingly gentle as they lathered her body, a stark contrast to the violence she knew lurked beneath the surface.

"My given name is Charles; Partlow is my surname," he whispered into her ear, his confession barely audible over the rush of water. His arms tightened around her waist, his mouth tracing along the curve of her shoulder. "And I have access to places no one else does."

The game was on, and Dawn was winning.

"I want to go down," she said playfully.

"Why ask? Just do it." He took a step back and began stroking his penis.

"No, you asshole. I want to see the sub-compound."

He agreed, surprised it was that simple, but with conditions—the powers that be demanded it.

THE SELECTION

They called it the Opportunity, but everyone knew it meant Selection.

It began the same every cycle—no explanation or warning, just inmates summoned over the intercom to proceed immediately to the infirmary. Those in the know understood: four to eight would enter, and only one would emerge.

Most of the names were nobodies this time, Groundsliders trying to rise in the ranks. But the fourth name stopped traffic.

Knight, Dawn.

Gasps spread like smoke. Eyes turned. Conversations halted.

Someone whispered, "She's going to the Arena."

NOTES TAKEN

The Compound's handlers watched from behind mirrored screens and video monitors. Her stats were off the charts—reflexes, efficiency, emotional control. More than that, she had a story. The watchers—clients who paid obscene fees to tune into the Compound's broadcast—were intrigued.

She was the rebel, the protector, the one who made mutants bleed.

It was time to test the myth.

But they weren't ready to throw her to Big Les yet.

First, they needed to measure audience loyalty—see if she could carry a fight, build tension, sell tickets.

That meant a trial match, a warm-up—something bloody, something visual, something broadcastable.

The guards began watching her more closely, whispering about a new slot in the under-card.

Her time was approaching. Soon, she'd be taken deep beneath the facility, where biometric locks and retina scans controlled entry to death as entertainment. Clients tuned in from across the world to watch

PRE-MATCH RITUAL

Selection Day was unlike anything Dawn had experienced. The prison shut down in silence. Hallways cleared. Inmates passed notes for information on the event as it slowly trickled through. Only chosen fighters moved, escorted through sterilized tunnels like prize cattle.

Her prep cell was clean and cold: a cot, a stack of gear, and a bottle of water she didn't trust.

A small, familiar voice came through the door. "You'll be facing Subject G-4."

Dawn frowned. Not a name—a classification. She rose from the cot as the door opened.

"Bambi!" She rushed into Dawn's arms like a child missing her mother.

"Where have you been? What happened?" Dawn couldn't contain her excitement.

"From the infirmary. Once I regained my strength, a guard pulled some strings and got me placed down here as a trustee. I had to get away from Les. She was going to kill me."

"I'm so happy you're alive and well. I couldn't get anyone to tell me anything; I was beginning to think you had died."

"That was Miller's idea—the guard. He saved me."

Their reunion and niceties, though sweet and emotional, would have to wait. Dawn cupped Bambi's face in her hands. She looked almost angelic now, healthy and glowing.

For the moment, she was safe.

ENTERING THE RING

Dawn dressed slowly: black cargo pants, reinforced boots, tactical gloves. No weapons.

The Arena wasn't a pit or ring but a cage designed to look like a prison cell, lowered onto a polished, multi-leveled combat floor surrounded by clear digital panels. It smelled like metal and adrenaline. Audience silhouettes shifted behind tinted glass. Dozens of them.

She could hear murmurs, the hum of drones above, a pulsing bass track playing like a heartbeat.

Then the gate opened. She entered the cage and waited for her challenger.

G-4 emerged from the corridor opposite hers and made his way into the cage.

He was massive—close to seven feet tall, with muscles like corded wire. His skin shimmered unnaturally under the lights, hints of scale beneath his flesh. His eyes were milk-white, his breathing erratic.

Mutant. Drug-stabilized. Weaponized.

The voice in the arena boomed:

"Let the combat begin."

VITAL SIGNS

The fight was brutally violent and physically demanding. Blood was spilled, and Dawn drew it. Partlow's description of her movements was fitting—she was unbelievably fast and vicious, like a cat.

The rules were simple: fight like hell and don't die before the time ends. Winning survivors in need of care were treated in the medical facility on the lower level—top-tier compared to the butcher shop of the infirmary. As they healed, they were pampered and trained in relative luxury, an incentive for those who had experienced it to go above and beyond to maintain championship status at all costs.

This was how and why Big Les reigned.

Dawn didn't remember blacking out, but she woke strapped to a table.

The restraints were soft, medical-grade, but they meant one thing: she wasn't supposed to be unconscious. Her head ached, and her shoulder throbbed. The last thing she remembered was G-4's body hitting the floor with a wet thud—and the crowd's silence just before the system cut the feed.

Now... this.

White ceiling. White walls. Lights embedded like surgical instruments. The air smelled of antiseptic and electricity.

A voice hummed from the corner:

"Vitals stable. Neuroelectricity consistent with pre-match baseline. Cellular regeneration increased by 8.7 percent."

Dawn turned her head. A woman in a white coat stood behind a transparent data wall, scrolling through metrics with a fingertip.

Not a guard. Not a warden.

A doctor.

"Where am I?" Dawn asked, her voice dry.

The woman didn't look up. "MedOps Sub-Level 3. Designated Recovery and Optimization."

Dawn tugged at the restraints. "Those aren't necessary."

This time, the doctor looked up, eyes blank behind biometric contact lenses. "They're not for our safety," she said calmly. "They're for yours. Some patients… wake up different."

The restraints clicked open with a hiss.

Dawn sat up slowly, studying the room. Beyond the data wall, a corridor was lined with glass chambers. Inside: bodies. Unmoving. Wired. Monitored.

Fighters. Inmates. Some she recognized—others were twisted, half-healed monsters with viral mutations barely contained by sedation.

She swung her legs off the table. Two guards entered the room and stood near the door.

"What is this place?" she asked, noting their positions.

The doctor tapped the wall again. A profile appeared—Knight, Dawn. Status: Exceptional Response. Compatibility: Unknown. Authorization Pending.

"Recovery. Diagnostics. Observation," the woman replied flatly.

"Test subjects," Dawn said, not asking.

The doctor tilted her head. "That's one word for them. You're lucky. Most aren't conscious for this part."

A silent beat passed. Dawn's fists clenched reflexively.

"I'm not most," she said.

Dawn's breath was ragged from the fight, her knuckles raw, her shoulder dislocated then relocated mid-match. She'd expected stitches, painkillers, maybe a day in gen-pop isolation to let the bruising fade.

Instead, they took her somewhere she hadn't seen.

The doctor left as a nurse entered, approaching with a smile that didn't reach her eyes.

"You did well in the ring," the nurse said.

Dawn stood to leave.

The two guards stepped forward, hands on tranquilizers.

"You want to fight again, don't you?" the nurse asked. "That means staying healthy. And that means compliance."

A familiar voice entered the room. "Please be compliant. I'd hate to see things end. We've been getting along so well."

Dawn's subtle excitement slipped through her usual stoic indifference. "Partlow? What are you doing here?"

"I want to bring you back to our paradise." He walked into the annoyingly sterile room.

"But how?"

"The privileges of proper alliance. You'd be surprised how comfortable your existence here can be if you're willing to play along," Partlow murmured as he approached, greeting Dawn with a hug.

"I'm not one for games," she replied, melting into his arms.

"It's not so much a game as a way of securing comfort and survival."

BEHIND THE CURTAIN

As the nurse turned away, Dawn noticed a flicker of light under the door, a figure casting a shadow on the other side. The guard cracked it open. A man in a suit—too clean for this place—peeked in, watching.

He tapped something into a tablet, nodded once, handed it to Partlow, and walked away.

Dawn rose from the table. "Who was that? What's going on?"

"Your sponsor," Partlow replied. "You have one now."

"I didn't ask for one."

"They don't ask you. They choose."

Dawn's skin crawled.

"Incarceration here is a business," Partlow said firmly. "It's entertainment for the elites, the ultimate reality TV. We provide everything from sex to graphic violence. Being sponsored isn't a bad thing; it gives you amenities I don't even have."

Dawn stared, indifferent.

"Not everyone is given such a gift," he went on. "To be sponsored after just one fight? You put in one hell of a performance."

"So from one fight, I get carte blanche?" Dawn was skeptical, trying to connect the dots and get back on track with her mission.

"You fight like a blade trying to remember it was forged to kill," Partlow scolded. "If you're going to survive, you'd better let go of any high moral stance and become the animal those mutants are."

"You've seen me fight once, and you think you've figured me out?"

"Once is enough. For some, that's a death sentence. For others... an invitation. You're the new belle of the ball, and you happen to be with the undisputed king of this madhouse."

Dawn smiled half-heartedly. "So now you're royalty?"

"In this shithole, I'm the second-best thing to have by your side."

"Really, and what's the first?"

Partlow's face stiffened. "A gun."

A slow smile broke through as they both caught the humor, but their moment was cut short as the door hissed open. A pair of guards entered.

"We're here to escort you back to your floor," one said, addressing Partlow.

"So, will you be joining me?" Partlow reached for her hand. "I can't provide you the luxuries I'm sure they've prepared for their new top prospect, but I'd be honored if you give me the opportunity to try and impress you with the meager amenities my privilege affords me."

Dawn offered her hand—and a devilish smirk Partlow didn't miss.

"I just got a little twinkle in my nether regions," he whispered.

Dawn let out an uncontrollable burst of laughter that startled both guards.

The two emerged from the sublevels, greeted by Partlow's personal security detail—several of the biggest and most violent inmates, trustees, and guards—who ushered them through general population to a thunderous roar of mixed emotions.

Partlow had been seen as a violent tyrant with a long history of abuse and debauchery, but being seen with Dawn in such a carefree manner made many take notice—including Big Les.

SLOW BURN TO WAR

Les wouldn't strike right away. She watched Dawn, sizing her up, giving her nods in passing, sometimes even smiling or laughing as if privy to a secret joke. It was all part of a strategic game—chess without pieces or a board. Strategies of an impending war.

One Les looked forward to, either as a spectacle for the elites or within the blind spots of pathways and corridors, beyond the watchful eyes of guards and cameras. Spots often used for nefarious activities.

Activities Les—and many inmates and staff—knew all too well yet chose to ignore.

Les wondered how she would initiate the conflict, what trigger beyond the ring would ignite Dawn to action.

The answer arrived with Dawn's first summons to participate in the Arena as a rising contender. As on many prior occasions, Les did the preliminary exams, met with medical staff, was informed of her competitor, and upon demolishing her opponent, was offered the chance to relax in opulence befitting her title as champion.

It was during one such stretch of debauchery and abundance that she learned of Bambi's survival—and demanded her return.

It didn't take long; news traveled fast, especially when requested by someone like Les. She returned to gen-pop with her former prize in tow, a shell of her former self. Bambi was sent to Partlow's tier to deliver a message to Dawn.

Her appearance spoke volumes.

Dawn made her way to Partlow's guarded entrance and fought to conceal her shock at Bambi's horrific condition. A single tear rolled down Bambi's face when she saw Dawn. She collapsed into her bosom like a child to its mother, pressing a crumpled photo into Dawn's hand—herself before the pain, before the collar. Eyes bright. Smile real.

"She sees you as a threat, inside or outside the ring," Bambi whispered, her voice raw. "If it goes down outside the ring, know that you won't be alone."

Bambi was fading. She had obviously been abused by Big Les; her bruises weren't healing. Her voice had shrunk to a whisper, one eye swollen and still. The guards turned away. Such was the power of a high-revenue champion, and Les brought in more money than anyone.

"She's going to kill me soon," Bambi whispered. "Unless someone makes her stop."

Dawn didn't answer, but her jaw clenched.

TRAJECTORY

The line had been drawn.

Not by the mission.

Not by the Professor.

But by the soul of a girl no one else saw anymore.

And Dawn had never left a soul behind.

The contests continued, but few held as much prestige and interest as the impending battle between Les and Dawn. The energy inside the facility was electric. Les quickly defeated her combatants, going above and beyond to display lethal, unnecessary brutality.

Dawn showed no reaction to the taunts or gore. Entering the ring, she did the opposite of Les—displaying precision and technique, ending her matches in record time with minimal damage to herself or her opponents.

It created a ripple effect among the inmates, who mocked Les by pointing to their wrists—to mark how quickly Dawn finished her fights. Bambi, in an act of defiance, even joined the gesture, but not without consequences.

When Dawn heard, she refused to participate in her following matches, demanding they remove Bambi from Les's clutches and expedite their match.

Even Partlow petitioned on her behalf, but the schedule wouldn't be altered. The demand and tension drove profits through the roof. They wanted to prolong the finale as long as possible.

Days passed. Tensions escalated. Fights increased. Rumors spread of food tampering, water restriction, guard retaliation. But Dawn held steady, refusing to be provoked into reckless moves.

Then came the day Les spoke to her. No threats. No insults. Just a single line, delivered in passing: "They die for you now. That's cute."

Dawn heard the faint sound of doors closing in the distance. Somehow, the two of them had found themselves face-to-face in a rarely populated part of the facility—with no security cameras.

Then she remembered the message delivered by one of Partlow's guards—the same guard who had been escorting her and now had conveniently vanished. Partlow, forever the fixer...

Dawn yelled toward the direction of the closing door. "Tell him I said thank you!"

And with that outburst came the furious onslaught of a war machine—a beast forced for too long to leash her natural impulse to be ferocious, destructive, deliberate in dispensing obscene amounts of violence.

They would eventually find Big Les lying unconscious in a pool of her own blood in a cold, poorly lit, secluded hallway.

THE INEVITABLE

The Green Roof Garden sprawled above the prison like a hidden sanctuary, a stark contrast to the cold, lifeless stone of the penitentiary below. The air here was different, fresher, carrying the mingling scents of damp soil and blossoming flowers. Partlow found solace in this place, confiding in Dawn as they strolled through rows of leafy greens and vibrant flora. The warmth of the afternoon sun bathed them in golden hues, making the moment feel oddly serene despite the walls of confinement that loomed just beyond.

But the calm was fleeting.

As they re-entered his cell, the shift was sudden, jarring. Dawn's hand clamped around his arm with surprising strength, halting him. Wordlessly, she turned to face him, her eyes dark with an unreadable emotion. Then, slowly, she squatted before him, her lips parting in a playful, predatory manner as she mimed his crotch.

"Drop your pants, Mr. Partlow," she purred, her voice laced with mischief.

The wet sound of her tongue sliding over her palm sent a shiver through him before she wrapped her fingers around his hardening flesh. Her other hand went to her lips, sucking two fingers before sliding them between his legs.

"Spread your legs," she whispered, her breath warm against his skin.

A sharp intake of air was all the invitation she needed. Her fingers traced downward, teasing, probing, before invading. His breath hitched, a strangled sound escaping his throat as he adjusted to the invasive pleasure.

"You like that, don't you?" she said, her tone a mix of disgust and dominance.

"Yeah," he admitted, wincing as her movements grew bolder, pushing deeper, demanding more.

Her rhythm slowed only slightly as she continued, her voice laced with curiosity. "Charles, what did you do to get locked up?"

He gritted his teeth. "Don't stop—I'm almost there."

Dawn's fingers ceased instantly. "If you wanna cum, start talking."

His body tensed with frustration. "I'll tell you! Just don't stop, damn it!"

Silence. Then, a smirk curled her lips as she withdrew completely.

"What the fuck! You bitch, I said don't stop!" His voice thundered through the small cell, but Dawn simply straightened, staring down at him with that same knowing smile.

"You don't run shit here, mister," she said coolly, stepping toward his bed. Her fingers traced the hem of her shirt before peeling it away, slowly revealing her skin. "New game. My rules."

She lay back, sprawled across the thin mattress, arms stretched above her head in a display of utter control. She motioned for him to join her, an open invitation laced with unspoken conditions.

"I'm in the mood for a story," she mused. "I'm sure you have more than a few good ones."

He hesitated, but her allure was stronger than his pride. Sliding onto the bed, he settled beside her. Her head rested against his chest, fingers trailing down his abdomen, occasionally brushing against him—a reminder of what was to come, if she deemed his words worthy.

"So why don't they fuck with you?" she asked, tone light, almost teasing.

A slow, wicked grin spread across his face. "I used to be an Agency man. They believe I have information they want—undercover agents, ongoing operations, who's under surveillance. Plus, I'm well-connected."

"Well-connected how?" she pressed.

"The government won't touch me because I have an angel fighting to keep me alive. Her money, her influence, and our little deception keep them from bringing the hammer down."

Dawn tilted her head, her lips grazing his chest before she bit down—a sharp sting that made him suck in a breath. The reaction was immediate. She felt him harden, a physical response to both pain and pleasure.

"See, what they don't know is that she and I were a team," he continued, his voice dipping into something darker. "The whole thing started with her sick, demented ass. I was assigned to investigate a series of abductions, and my findings led me straight to her. But instead of turning her in, I saw an opportunity."

Dawn remained silent, her mind racing. If his so-called angel was who she suspected—Ryne Lawson—then Partlow's connection to the recent abductions was far more significant than she had anticipated.

"I've heard about those murders," she said, feigning admiration. "You're famous."

The flattery worked. He basked in it, continuing his confession with a sickening sense of pride. He spoke of their years-long killing spree, their descent into human trafficking, how Lawson's wealth was built on organized crime and corruption. As the words tumbled from his lips, something inside him cracked. An unexpected wave of emotion overtook him. He laughed. He cried. The release was overwhelming.

Dawn watched him with careful calculation. "Are you alright?" she asked as he sat up, breath ragged, his face streaked with tears but stretched into a blissful smile.

"I feel wonderful," he murmured, rising from the bed and moving toward the bars. The setting sun cast long shadows across the walls, bathing the cell in an eerie orange glow. He looked toward the horizon, as if savoring his moment of liberation, however fleeting.

Dawn approached from behind, pressing a soft kiss against his bare back. "That's good," she whispered.

He turned, their eyes locking. She lifted her hands, trailing them up his shoulders, his neck, his face—tender, reverent. His grip on her waist tightened as he leaned in for a kiss.

Then, in a blur of motion, she struck. One hand snapped to his chin, the other to the back of his head.

The sickening crack of his neck shattered the silence.

His body crumpled instantly, hitting the floor like a marionette with its strings cut.

Dawn exhaled, rolling her shoulders as she stepped over him. The job was done.

She never played a game she didn't intend to win.

***

Moments later, Dawn emerged from Partlow's cell, the heavy door sliding shut behind her with ominous finality. She adjusted her clothing with deliberate movements, her expression unreadable, her breath steady despite the turmoil within. The dim corridor stretched before her like an endless abyss.

Then she noticed the approaching figure—a guard. Her pulse quickened, but she maintained her composure. As their eyes met, recognition flickered.

It was Miller. The same guard who had led her from solitary, the same man who had stood silently in the shadows watching her first harrowing encounter with Partlow. There was something different in his gaze now—an unspoken allegiance.

He approached without hesitation, his boots barely making a sound. In his hands, he carried a pillowcase, weighted with unseen but lethal contents. He halted inches from her, his voice a low murmur as he extended it.

"Compliments of the Professor," he whispered. "You have ten minutes to get to the roof."

Dawn curled her fingers around the rough fabric, her sharp eyes scanning his face for any trace of deception.

"Why are you doing this?" she asked, her voice a blend of skepticism and curiosity.

Miller's jaw tightened as he weighed his words. "Let's just say I owe the Professor a debt," he admitted, his voice barely audible over the hum of fluorescent lights. "And I've seen enough of Partlow's evil to last a lifetime. He had good reason for wanting him gone."

Understanding flickered in Dawn's gaze. The Professor was not a man who acted without purpose, and Miller's unexpected assistance was another calculated piece in his intricate game.

"What about you?" she asked. "What happens to you once I'm gone?"

Miller exhaled slowly, a rueful smile tugging at the corner of his lips. "I've made my peace with whatever comes," he said, his tone laced with resignation. "Just make sure Partlow doesn't get another chance to spread his sickness. That'll be enough for me."

Dawn's expression softened, an unspoken gratitude passing between them. "I won't forget this," she said, her voice steady.

Miller gave a curt nod. "Just go. And good luck."

As she turned, his voice stopped her.

"One more thing. The Professor left you a message."

Dawn tensed. "What is it?"

His voice dropped to a whisper. "'The sins of the father must not be visited upon the son.'"

The words slid down her spine, cold as steel—a warning, a plea, a trap.

"What does that mean?" she asked.

Miller shook his head. "I don't know. But he said you would."

She lingered for a heartbeat, then slipped into the shadows, her footfalls silent. Miller watched her disappear, knowing he'd sealed his own fate. The walls of this prison had swallowed better men, and he had no illusions about what awaited him once the higher-ups discovered his betrayal. But it was a choice he could live with.

Dawn moved with purpose, every step driven by the knowledge that time was against her. She reached into the pillowcase and pulled out the tools of her escape—semi-automatic weapons, explosives, a coil of thick rope. Their weight was reassuring, a silent promise that she would not leave defenseless.

Her path was set. She turned toward the stairwell that led to the roof, her fingers tightening around the weapons.

Then she hesitated.

Bambi.

Dawn's breath hitched. Without another moment's hesitation, she pivoted, heading toward the infirmary. She had come this far. She wouldn't leave without knowing if Bambi had survived.

Time was slipping through her fingers. But for Bambi, she was willing to risk it all.

Dawn burst through the double doors of the prison infirmary, her breath coming in sharp bursts, her eyes wild with urgency. The sterile stench of antiseptic and the low hum of medical monitors permeated the air, but she barely noticed. She demanded answers, only to be met with the infuriating truth—against medical advice, the warden had ordered Bambi back to her cell under the care of her cellmate, Big Les.

Dawn's heart clenched. Big Les had just been released from the infirmary after their brutal encounter. Now, Bambi was nothing more than sustenance for her mutation.

"She needs Bambi to feed on," Dawn seethed internally.

Her fists clenched as she turned and bolted out of the infirmary, her footsteps echoing down the desolate corridor. Every muscle in her body coiled with tension, her mind consumed with a singular focus. She needed to reach Big Les before it was too late.

She moved like a specter through the prison's winding corridors, her shadow flickering against the dim walls. She avoided unnecessary skirmishes, slipping past inattentive guards and weaving through the labyrinth with practiced precision. But confrontation was inevitable. A group of guards stepped into her path, hands on their weapons.

"I don't have time for this," Dawn muttered.

Before they could react, she struck. A calculated series of swift, precise blows sent them collapsing to the ground, unconscious. She stepped over their bodies without breaking stride.

At last, she reached her destination. The heavy steel door to Bambi's cell loomed before her, slightly ajar. A sickly scent—a mixture of sweat and something primal—hung in the air. Dawn pushed the door open, her breath hitching at the sight.

Big Les knelt over Bambi's limp form, her hulking frame eclipsing the smaller woman. Her head was buried between Bambi's legs, but this was no act of intimacy—Bambi's skin was deathly pale, her body unnaturally still.

"You weren't infected. You're one of the original Hundred," Dawn announced, leveling her weapon.

Big Les straightened slowly, her massive shoulders rising and falling with labored breaths. Her back remained to Dawn, but there was no need for words—Dawn knew exactly what was happening. Les was feeding, drawing life from Bambi to fuel the mutation that had corrupted her.

"I'd love to engage you," Dawn continued coolly, "but I'm on a schedule."

With a guttural snarl, Big Les turned, her transformation incomplete yet already grotesque. Her body expanded, muscles straining beneath her skin, veins bulging. Her breath came in ragged, animalistic gasps.

Dawn did not hesitate.

Four shots. Each precise. Each final.

The monstrous woman staggered, struggling to continue her transformation, her chest heaving in desperate gulps. Her breaths grew shorter, more erratic, until they ceased altogether.

The body hit the ground with a sickening thud. For a moment, the only sound was the heavy rasp of Dawn's breathing.

She stepped over the corpse and knelt beside Bambi. The woman's skin was ice cold. Her eyes, once full of mischief and fire, were now vacant. Dawn clenched her jaw, fury boiling over. With a sharp exhale, she drove her foot into the lifeless skull of Big Les, her frustration reverberating through the cell.

Without another glance, she turned and stormed out.

Then—something shifted. A mechanical whir. A low, guttural thrum above.

She lifted her gaze.

Above the prison, a black helicopter cut through the night sky, its silhouette swallowing the stars.

On the watchtowers, sharpshooters hurried into position, rifles trained on the airborne intruder.

"She's not going to make it. We have to leave!" the pilot barked, his voice tense.

His passenger, a man with sharp, calculating eyes, leaned forward, gripping the dashboard. "One more pass over the Green Roof," he demanded.

The pilot gritted his teeth but obeyed. As they swung low, the towers erupted with gunfire. Guards poured onto the Green Roof, weapons raised. The passenger's expression darkened.

"Take offensive measures. Shoot down Tower One."

A missile streaked from the helicopter, striking the structure with devastating force. The explosion sent debris raining down, guards scattering in terror. Flames licked the night sky as smoke billowed upward.

"What about the rooftop?" the pilot pressed.

"She'll make it," the passenger assured. "We have to give her more time."

Below, chaos reigned. More guards flooded the yard, bullets whizzing through the air, some striking the chopper.

"We can't take much more of this, sir!" the pilot swore.

The passenger did not hesitate. He drew his own weapon and returned fire, his shots finding their marks with ruthless efficiency. "Hold here. Just a few more seconds."

Then, as if on cue, guards on the rooftop began to fall—one by one, taken out from behind. A blur of motion burst from the stairwell, carving through them with lethal precision.

Dawn had arrived.

"It's Dawn! Take it down, now, damn it!"

She sprinted across the rooftop, dodging stray bullets as she made her way toward the far edge, away from the yard. The helicopter swooped in, hovering just within reach.

Without breaking stride, Dawn leaped, her fingers locking around the landing gear. The chopper tilted, ascending rapidly as more guards spilled onto the roof, their gunfire relentless.

The wind roared in her ears as the rooftop dropped away beneath her. A bullet whizzed past—too close—searing a line of heat along her shoulder.

The helicopter hovered just out of reach. Too far. Too fast.

No time to think.

She ran. Pushed harder. At the last possible moment, she launched herself into the air.

For a breathless instant—nothing. Just weightlessness. The void yawning beneath her.

Then—impact. Cold metal against her palms. Her fingers slipped, grasped, then locked onto the landing gear. Her breath hitched as she dangled, her legs kicking over empty space.

The chopper tilted. Gunfire erupted from the rooftop.

Clenching her teeth, she swung herself up, one arm looping over the frame as she twisted, her gun raised. Two shots. Two guards down. The others scattered as the prison fell away beneath her.

A strong arm reached down to pull her up. To her surprise, it was Matthew. Their eyes met, locking in silent recognition. No words were exchanged, but the understanding between them was undeniable.

"Welcome aboard, ma'am," the pilot called back, relief evident in his voice.

Dawn exhaled heavily, her pulse still racing. Below them, the prison faded into the darkness.

Their next stop—safe haven.

22 NIGHT BREED BEGINS

Dawn awoke in a cold sweat, her breath ragged, heart pounding against her ribs. The nightmare still clung to her—a grotesque tableau of twisted figures warped by viral mutation, eyes glowing with predatory hunger that sent a shiver down her spine. Even in the safety of her apartment, the echoes of the dream wrapped around her like an icy shroud.

She pushed herself up from the bed, running a trembling hand through sweat-dampened hair. The sleek, minimalist lines of her apartment—usually a bastion of order and control—felt strangely cold and impersonal in the dim glow of the city skyline. The Secure Cities— her supposed haven—felt more like a gilded cage, a fragile illusion of safety. Fifteen years she had spent forging this life, distancing herself from the blood-soaked past of Agent A-10, the lethal operative of Gen X. But the past was relentless. It did not forget, and it did not forgive.

With a deep breath, she swung her legs over the edge of the bed and padded toward the bathroom. The reflection in the mirror was both familiar and alien—sharp emerald eyes, high cheekbones, the athletic frame that had once made her a formidable assassin. But something was off. A flicker of unease danced in her expression, a subtle tension tightening her features. Beneath her skin, a foreign sensation coiled like a sleeping beast, waiting to awaken.

She could feel it—the virus stirring within her veins.

"Damn it," she muttered, splashing cold water onto her face, willing the changes to halt. The metamorphosis was beginning again.

The sharp chime of her secure comm cut through the silence, making her stiffen. Wiping her face with a towel, she turned as the screen flickered to life. The Professor's face appeared, brow furrowed, the ever-present shadow of worry lining his aging features.

"Dawn," he said, voice low and urgent. "I know you felt it."

She exhaled, leaning against the sink. "It's getting worse, Professor."

He didn't hesitate. "The injection—"

"—was only partially effective," she finished, frustration tightening her voice.

The Professor's expression remained solemn. "I won't lie to you, Dawn. There were risks. But based on the data, we had a sixty-percent chance of neutralizing the toxins."

She let out a dry laugh. "So I'm still prone to changing. Fantastic."

His gaze softened, but his words stayed firm. "Unlike the others, you remain in control. They… weren't as fortunate. The virus twisted them beyond recognition—mutated, disfigured, driven to madness. You are not them."

Dawn ran a hand through her hair, frustration simmering beneath her carefully maintained composure. "How often is this going to happen? What triggers it?"

The Professor sighed, fingers steepled. "I don't know yet, but I'm working on it." His tone sharpened. "Until then, you need to hold it together. Understood?"

She bristled but nodded. The stakes were too high for defiance. The Professor needed her—and she needed him. He was the key to unlocking the truth about her past, her present, and possibly her future.

"What is it?" she asked, bracing herself.

"The abductions," he said grimly. "They're escalating. Whoever's behind them is getting bolder, and I believe they're connected to something much bigger than random acts of violence."

Dawn's pulse quickened. The past was calling her back, dragging her into the shadows she had fought so hard to escape. Some battles never truly ended—and some wars were never meant to be won.

DESCENT

The dim overhead lamp cast long shadows across the cluttered mahogany desk, the only light in the Professor's vast study. Bookshelves lined the walls, filled with arcane and illicit knowledge, secrets hoarded over the years. The air was heavy with aged paper and cigar smoke, hinting at the weight of matters discussed within these walls.

Tonight was no different.

Dawn awoke in a cold sweat, her breath ragged, her heart pounding against her ribs. The nightmare still clung to her—a grotesque tableau of twisted figures warped by viral mutation, their eyes glowing with predatory hunger that sent a shiver down her spine. Even in the safety of her apartment, the echoes of the dream wrapped around her like an icy shroud.

She pushed herself up from the bed, running a trembling hand through sweat-dampened hair. The sleek, minimalist lines of her apartment—usually a bastion of order and control—felt strangely cold and impersonal in the dim glow of the city skyline. The Secure Cities— her supposed haven—felt more like a gilded cage, a fragile illusion of safety. Fifteen years she had spent forging this life, distancing herself from the blood-soaked past of Agent A-10, the lethal operative of Gen X. But the past was relentless. It did not forget, and it did not forgive.

With a deep breath, she swung her legs over the edge of the bed and padded toward the bathroom. The reflection in the mirror was both familiar and alien—sharp emerald eyes, high cheekbones, the athletic frame that had once made her a formidable assassin. But something was off. A flicker of unease danced in her expression, a subtle tension tightening her features. Beneath her skin, a foreign sensation coiled like a sleeping beast, waiting to awaken.

She could feel it—the virus stirring within her veins.

"Damn it," she muttered, splashing cold water onto her face, willing the changes to halt. The metamorphosis was beginning again.

The sharp chime of her secure comm cut through the silence, making her stiffen. Wiping her face with a towel, she turned as the screen flickered to life. The Professor's face appeared, his brow furrowed, the ever-present shadow of worry lining his aging features.

"Dawn," he said, his voice low and urgent. "I know you felt it."

She exhaled, leaning against the sink. "It's getting worse, Professor."

He didn't hesitate. "The injection—"

"—was only partially effective," she finished, frustration tightening her voice.

The Professor's expression remained solemn. "I won't lie to you, Dawn. There were risks. But based on the data, we had a sixty-percent chance of neutralizing the toxins."

She let out a dry laugh. "So I'm still prone to changing. Fantastic."

His gaze softened, but his words stayed firm. "Unlike the others, you remain in control. They... weren't as fortunate. The virus twisted them beyond recognition—mutated, disfigured, driven to madness. You are not them."

Dawn ran a hand through her hair, frustration simmering beneath her carefully maintained composure. "How often is this going to happen? What triggers it?"

The Professor sighed, his fingers steepled. "I don't know yet, but I'm working on it." His tone sharpened. "Until then, you need to hold it together. Understood?"

She bristled but nodded. The stakes were too high for defiance. The Professor needed her—and she needed him. He was the key to unlocking the truth about her past, her present, and possibly her future.

"What is it?" she asked, bracing herself.

"The abductions," he said grimly. "They're escalating. Whoever's behind them is getting bolder, and I believe they're connected to something much bigger than random acts of violence."

Dawn's pulse quickened. The past was calling her back, dragging her into the shadows she had fought so hard to escape. Some battles never truly ended—and some wars were never meant to be won.

DESCENT

The dim overhead lamp cast long shadows across the cluttered mahogany desk, the only light in the Professor's vast study. Bookshelves lined the walls, filled with arcane and illicit knowledge—secrets hoarded over the years. The air was heavy with aged paper and cigar smoke, hinting at the weight of matters discussed within these walls.

Tonight was no different.

The Professor leaned forward, his steely eyes narrowing as he outlined the mission. A wave of abductions had rattled Secure City 24, confounding the authorities. Young women vanishing without a trace, their names becoming whispers in back alleys and late-night broadcasts. But he knew better. This was not the work of common criminals. The pattern was too deliberate, too methodical. He suspected the sinister hand of the Outer World's underbelly—the sprawling, insidious network of the sex-slave trade.

Dawn sat opposite him, her arms crossed, her face an unreadable mask. "Why is this case of such interest to you? How does stopping this help our cause?" she asked, skeptical.

The Professor exhaled slowly, his fingertips pressing together before he answered. "It's about networking, Dawn. One hand washes the other." His voice was calm and measured, yet undercut with revulsion barely kept in check. "We have friends in high places, individuals with unsavory appetites. They indulge in things they shouldn't, hidden behind veils of wealth and power. And then we have those who think themselves untouchable, who believe they can push the limits further. Both disgust me, but for now, it's a game of control—the lesser of evils when you consider the bigger picture."

Dawn's fingers tightened on the armrests, but she said nothing.

"In time, they will all be dealt with," he went on. "But for now, we have an ally who has lost something precious. A young college student vanished weeks ago—a very special girl, the daughter of one of these corrupt, influential men." He smirked, humorless. "He kept her under tight protection, but you know how the young are. She thought she could outsmart the system, swapping IDs and dorm rooms with another student. And just like that—gone. Abducted. Forced into the Outer World's underground market." He let the irony linger. "Fitting, isn't it? The hunter's own kin caught in the snare."

Dawn's stomach churned. The Outer World was a festering wound, a place where humanity rotted from the inside out. Disease, depravity, and despair festered in its streets like an unchecked infection—a place she had hoped never to return to.

"You want me to go back out there?" she asked, her voice flat as a blade.

"I know what I'm asking," the Professor admitted, his voice softening for the first time. "But this isn't just about one girl. This is about sending a message, about disrupting the balance of power. And you are the only one who can do it."

The weight of his words settled over her like a shroud. Her assignment: infiltrate the operation, slipping into the role of a submissive under the guise of servitude. She would work under a madam—a woman who straddled the line between the Outer World's grim underbelly and the polished elite of Secure City 24. She would have to become one of them, blend into the filth, all while searching for the girl.

She exhaled sharply, pushing back the dread curling in her gut. "Fine. But only on one condition."

The Professor raised an eyebrow. "Name it."

"Matthew is my handler."

The room fell silent. The Professor's jaw tightened, a flicker of hesitation crossing his face. He considered her for a long moment before exhaling.

"Very well," he conceded, reluctance clinging to his words like tar.

Dawn's heart pounded as she nodded. The deal was struck. There was no turning back.

A dilapidated safehouse loomed on the outskirts of Secure City, standing defiantly against the encroaching wilderness of the Outer World. The air inside was thick with tension, mingling with the faint scent of dust and aged wood. The sparse furnishings—a battered sofa, a rickety table, a dimly flickering overhead light—did little to make the place inviting. Yet for Matthew and Dawn, it was their only sanctuary before the chaos to come.

They huddled together, scrutinizing a worn map spread across the table, hashing out a questionable plan to infiltrate a brazen trafficking organization thriving in the lawless expanse beyond the city. The lack of intel and the inability to communicate once the mission began gnawed at Matthew. The clock on the wall ticked methodically, each second chipping away at the time left before Dawn disappeared into danger again.

Frustration welled in his throat until he could no longer hold it back. "I hate this!" he burst out, his voice laced with fury. His training dictated control, but emotion surged past his discipline. "It's like he deliberately keeps us apart. Either I'm rotting in some godforsaken hole, or he has you risking your life for reasons I can't even begin to understand!"

Dawn remained composed, her demeanor unwavering. She stepped closer, a smirk curling at the edges of her lips. "I know it seems pointless at times, but we have to stay optimistic," she purred, her fingers trailing teasingly down his chest before stopping just below his belt. "Besides, absence makes the heart grow fonder." Her hand moved lower, a playful glint in her eyes. "And absence makes the dick grow harder."

Matthew exhaled sharply, a begrudging smile tugging at his lips. "So this is how you change the subject?"

"Is it working?"

The growing tightness in his pants answered for him. She watched as he unbuckled his belt, his expression shifting from frustration to something far more primal.

"Why do you always protect him?" Matthew's voice was quiet but sharp, edged with longing and betrayal. "After everything he's done... how can you still trust him?"

Dawn stiffened. The room suddenly felt too small.

"I don't trust him," she said finally. "But I understand him."

Matthew let out a harsh breath. "That's not the same thing, Dawn."

"No, it's not," she admitted. "But sometimes, understanding a monster is the only way to survive it."

He shook his head, stepping back like he needed space. "I hate that he still owns a piece of you."

"He doesn't," she said—and even as she said it, she wasn't sure it was true.

Her only response was to lower herself in front of him. "Do you really want to have this conversation right now?" she asked, brushing her face across his groin. "Or would you rather I do something far more enjoyable with my mouth?"

Whatever objections Matthew might have had dissolved as the night stretched on, their bodies entwining again and again until sleep finally overtook them.

The dream came in fragmented flashes—his hands, his voice, the press of his body against hers. The first time. Or countless others.

23 NIGHTS WITH THE PROFESSOR

Dawn jolted awake, her heart hammering. Sweat clung to her skin despite the cool air of the motel room. She slipped quietly out of bed and staggered to the bathroom, gripping the sink as she stared at her reflection.

"It's not real," she whispered, searching for something—anything— in her own eyes that belonged to her and not to him.

The memories felt too real, too vivid to be dreams. Yet there was a detachment, a sense of something foreign—something implanted.

Had it always been her desire? Or had he crafted it within her mind, just as he had crafted her past?

A past that gnawed at the edges of her thoughts. The way his voice had curled around her name. The way she had obeyed, without understanding why.

Her breath hitched, nausea rising. No. No more.

She couldn't remember ever having feelings for him—not like these. What she and Matthew had was real. The other defied description, a sickening footnote to a chapter she had already closed.

She had to end this. And to do that, she'd have to confront him.

She splashed her face with water and returned to bed, finding Matthew awake and waiting for her. "You okay, babe? Bad dream?" he asked softly, his voice laced with familiar warmth.

Dawn nodded. "How'd you guess?" She hated showing weakness, especially to Matthew.

He reached for her, pulling her into his arms. "I don't sleep that hard. I felt you flinching." He held her close, his strong arms enveloping her. "It's okay," he murmured, stroking her hair. "You're safe now."

Morning arrived with a muted quiet.

Dawn moved stealthily as she rose from the bed, making her way through the safe house and slipping outside with Matthew's SAT communication device.

Nervous anticipation tightened her chest as she waited for it to connect. The screen flickered, and the Professor's voice came first, edged with annoyance.

"Confirm ID."

Dawn's voice came out soft, subservient. "Dawn, A-10, Gen-X."

He heard her and instantly appeared on screen. "Hey."

But Dawn had no patience for pleasantries. "You tampered with me," she said, her voice a blade sharpened by the weight of realization.

His lips curved in that maddening, knowing smile. "I created you."

"You made me into a killer. Fine. But did you also make me want you?"

The Professor tilted his head, as if genuinely considering the question. "Is it so unthinkable that desire is part of your design? After all, what is seduction but another weapon in an assassin's arsenal?"

Dawn's breath hitched, rage battling something deeper, something darker. "You made me need you."

His eyes softened, a rare flicker of something almost human. "I made you extraordinary. And you were never alone in this, Dawn. That feeling—the craving—it was real."

She wanted to hit him, to tear him apart for every moment she had spent questioning her own mind and desires. But worse than the rage, worse than the betrayal, was the terrifying truth that some part of her still ached for him.

And that, she realized, was his greatest triumph.

She muttered under her breath, barely audible even to herself. "You're such an asshole."

"An asshole?" he echoed, staring at her smugly. "When this assignment ends, come see me."

She felt a tightening in her stomach. "Yes, sir."

24 TORN AND TORMENTED

The first rays of daylight filtered through the dust-covered blinds. The smell of coffee mingled with the remnants of their night together. Matthew stirred from restless sleep, the rustling of maps and the metallic clink of weapons drawing him from his haze.

He blinked, adjusting to the sight of Dawn standing over the table, focused entirely on preparing for her departure.

"Good morning, early bird," he murmured, stretching lazily.

Dawn turned, an amused glimmer in her eyes. "Good morning, sleepyhead," she teased, then walked into the makeshift kitchen. She poured him a cup of coffee and handed it over, watching as he took a slow sip, blowing into the steaming liquid.

"I don't want to hear that word again until you get back," he muttered.

Dawn giggled. "Which word? Good? Morning? Sleepy? Or head?"

Matthew groaned, shaking his head with a smirk. "How did I get so lucky? Not only are you beautiful, but you're so silly... and a freak."

"Ditto, sir." She leaned in, her voice dropping to a sultry whisper. "If memory serves me right, you put in some serious mouth service last night. Thanks for the swirl, Mr. Perl Tongue."

They shared a lingering kiss, the humor between them briefly easing the weight of what was coming. But as Matthew's gaze fell back to the map, reality pressed in again. He sighed, his expression darkening.

"Don't worry, baby, I'll be alright," Dawn reassured him, but he barely seemed to hear.

"Do you think he knows?" he asked after a beat.

"Probably. And if he does, I don't give a shit."

Matthew's jaw tightened. "He can't keep me from seeing you. I'll always find a way to have eyes on you."

Dawn arched an eyebrow. "You sound like him. Are there cams in my place? Have you been…?"

"Yes and yes." He pulled her close, his voice dropping to something almost desperate. "I've almost lost you too many times to count. You have no idea what that's like."

Dawn's playful demeanor faltered. "Are you serious? I have no idea what that's like? I thought you were dead, Matthew."

A shadow crossed his face. "Oh… yeah. My bad. I forgot." He chuckled dryly, then sobered. "But you almost died too. Do you even know how long you were unconscious after those mutants got to you?"

Dawn frowned. "A couple days? A week, maybe?"

"Try three months."

Her breath hitched.

"The Professor put you in an induced coma to spare you the pain while your body fought off whatever the hell that antiviral concoction did," Matthew went on, his voice thick with unwanted memories. "I was there the whole time."

"I had no idea," Dawn whispered.

"No one thought you'd make it. The night sweats, the high fevers, the convulsions… and the metamorphosis."

Dawn's brows knitted. "Metamorphosis?"

Matthew nodded. "You kept changing. One moment, your complexion was dark chocolate, the next, caramel. You even got buff once—really buff."

"Like… a man?" Alarm crept into her voice.

"Not like a man," he assured her. "But definitely a strong-ass woman. You shrank at one point, then grew tall as hell. And your tits…"

Dawn crossed her arms. "Let me guess. They changed size?"

Matthew grinned. "Massively."

She rolled her eyes. "And let me also guess… you enjoyed it."

"It was fascinating! They got huge, but still firm. It was amazing."

Her eyes narrowed. "And how exactly do you know they were firm? Did you feel me up while I was in a coma?"

Matthew smirked, unrepentant. "I didn't take any pictures, if that's what you're asking." He paused. "But yeah… I copped a feel."

Dawn studied him for a long moment before laughing. "I don't give a FUUUCK. I'm just glad you enjoyed my big mutant titties. Just know, if you're ever in a coma, I'm grinding one out on your face."

The fragile moment of shared vulnerability and humor dissipated as they turned back to the map—a tattered, well-worn relic of past excursions through the underground tunnels. By the dim glow of a flickering lantern, they traced jagged routes that snaked beneath the city's foundation, hidden arteries connecting the relative safety of civilization to the chaos beyond. Shadows wavered against crumbling brick as they discussed the time to navigate the labyrinth, the hazards lurking in the dark, the firepower she would need, and the desperate contingencies if things went sideways.

Despite the meticulous planning, none of it gave Matthew any confidence in the Professor's decision. His jaw tightened, frustration bubbling beneath the surface.

"I know he's my dad, but he's a dick for this!" Matthew blurted, his voice cutting through the stillness.

Dawn let out a small, weary laugh, though her eyes betrayed the storm within. They embraced, holding each other as if memorizing the shape of the other's presence, knowing this might be their last moment together. When they finally pulled away, their eyes remained locked in silent understanding. With a soft smirk, Dawn blew him a kiss, grabbed a backpack, and disappeared into the shadows of the safehouse.

An hour and forty-six minutes later, the city loomed before her, a monument of abandonment and quiet menace. Dawn stepped out of an old elevator shaft hidden within a derelict subway station, the scent of mildew and rust thick in the stagnant air. Her boots barely made a sound against cracked pavement as she advanced, every step an exercise in caution.

The deeper she moved into the city's corpse, the clearer the evidence of its demise became—burned-out husks of vehicles, skeletal remains of once-bustling buildings, and an eerie silence that pressed against her like an unseen force. Humanity had left its scars here, and time had only deepened the wounds.

A faint buzzing broke the quiet. Dawn sought cover, then realized a small drone hovered overhead. As it descended, she saw an attached note: *I told you, I'd always have my eyes on you.*

She smiled, but annoyance prickled. How was he tracking her? She tore through the backpack, which should have held only weapons, snacks, a toothbrush, and clothing. Deeper inside, she found the device, removed it, and permanently dismantled it.

Guided by the Professor's cryptic instructions, she arrived at the agreed-upon meeting place—a strip mall ravaged by decay, its storefronts shattered, its walls blanketed in graffiti and the whisper of old memories. In the slanted glow of a flickering neon sign, she spotted him.

Sal was exactly as described—greasy, nervous, and reeking of cheap liquor and bad decisions. His wiry frame shuddered as he stepped out of the shadows, his eyes darting as if expecting trouble to emerge from the cracks in the concrete.

"You the broad the Professor sent?" he rasped, his voice thick with years of smoke and regret. He wiped his mouth with a stained handkerchief, doing little to disguise his desperation. "He said you were... special."

Dawn met his gaze, her expression unreadable, her hand instinctively grazing the Glock beneath her jacket. "Just tell me what I need to know."

A sly smirk crept onto Sal's face, though it never reached his eyes. "Looking for the Madam, are we? That kind of access comes at a price, doll. Information ain't free in this town."

Dawn's patience thinned. "I'm sure the Professor handled it. I don't like being played. Lead me to her, or you'll find out just how special I truly am."

Sal swallowed hard, his Adam's apple bobbing, then nodded. "There's a woman—calls herself Madame Evangeline. Runs a tight ship, caters to the high rollers in the Secure Cities. She's always looking for fresh talent."

With a hesitant glance over his shoulder, Sal led her through the skeletal remains of the city, weaving through back alleys and abandoned streets until they reached the outskirts. The warehouse stood like a fortress of forgotten vice, its rusted exterior concealing the sins within.

Sal stopped abruptly, shuffling backward as if unwilling to take another step. He lifted a trembling hand, gesturing toward the entrance. "The place is called the Inferno. That's where Evangeline does her recruiting. Be careful, lady. That place is a viper's nest. And Evangeline…" His voice dropped to a near whisper. "She's got teeth."

Dawn offered a curt nod, acknowledging his warning. Without hesitation, she stepped forward, slipping into the night.

The Inferno lived up to its name. The air was thick with sweat, smoke, and something far more illicit. Music pulsed through the walls, a chaotic rhythm of desperation and indulgence. Voices rose and fell— some in laughter, others in anger—all lost in the din of revelry and ruin. The entrance loomed before her, a gate to another world.

Dawn took a steadying breath, pushing away the razor-sharp instincts that made her a hunter. Tonight, she wasn't Dawn Knight, the Gen X assassin. That woman had no place here.

Instead, she let herself melt into someone new—someone desperate, overlooked, easily forgotten.

Who that would be, she had yet to decide. But she had a feeling she wouldn't have much time to figure it out.

She ducked into a secluded, darkened corner, changed clothes from her backpack, then stashed it.

THE VIPER'S NEST

The air inside the Inferno pulsed with an eerie electricity, an intoxicating mixture of anticipation and underlying menace. The warehouse, once a desolate industrial relic, had been reborn into a decadent labyrinth of vice and indulgence. Plush velvet couches sprawled across the dimly lit space, their rich fabrics absorbing the flashing neon hues from overhead lights. Mirrored walls reflected the depravity of its patrons—distorted images of men and women lost to hedonistic excess. The air was thick with expensive perfume, sweat, and the acrid bite of cigarettes, all blending into the unmistakable scent of desperation.

At the heart of the chaos, the dance floor writhed like a living, breathing entity. Guests—a tangled mix of the Secure City's wealthiest elite and hardened Outer World criminals—moved in a drug-fueled frenzy, bodies slick with perspiration as they surrendered to the throbbing bass. The boundaries between pleasure and peril blurred with every stolen glance, every whispered deal sealed in the shadows. The Inferno pulsed with heat and hunger.

Dawn moved through the crowd, sharp and unseen, her mission thrumming beneath her skin. Somewhere in this chaos, the missing student waited.

She played her role flawlessly, a delicate lamb descending into the lion's den, her wide eyes a perfect mask of innocence. Yet beneath the calm exterior, tension coiled like a serpent, ready to strike.

Above it all, from her throne of velvet and smoke, Madame Evangeline watched.

Her presence was calculated allure—tall and statuesque, draped in crimson silk that clung to her figure like liquid fire. Raven hair was pulled into a severe bun, accentuating the chiseled angles of her face. Her lips, painted the deep red of fresh blood, curled into a knowing smile, though her dark, glittering eyes remained cold and unreadable. She was the puppet master, delicately tugging at the strings of desire and despair alike.

Dawn made her way to the bar, acutely aware of hungry eyes tracking her every move. She was a newborn fawn, trembling and lost in a predator's den, yet none dared make the first move—not while the true alpha prowled. Madame Evangeline descended from her perch with the slow, deliberate grace of a huntress who had already decided to claim her prize.

Dawn steeled herself, inhaling deeply before softening her expression, outwardly surrendering to Evangeline's advance. "Madame Evangeline?" she murmured, her voice barely above a whisper, feigning the hesitance of an inexperienced girl in over her head. "I was told you might be… looking for someone."

The Madame's gaze swept over Dawn like a caress and a scalpel, assessing, dissecting. Interest flickered briefly, but her air of dismissiveness remained. "I'm always looking, darling," she purred, bringing a cigarette to her lips and taking a slow drag. "But I doubt you have what I need." With a calculated exhale, she sent a plume of smoke into Dawn's face, testing her.

Dawn didn't flinch. She met Evangeline's gaze head-on, her resolve unwavering. "I'm willing to do whatever it takes."

A slow, predatory smile curled along Evangeline's lips. "Whatever it takes?" she echoed, amusement and curiosity warring in her voice. "Those are dangerous words in this world, child. Tell me… what are you running from?"

A hesitation—brief, but intentional. Dawn spun her web of lies: desperation and betrayal, a shattered life. She painted herself as a victim, a woman with nothing left to lose. Every word was carefully chosen, a calculated lure cast into the abyss.

Evangeline listened in silence, her expression a masterpiece of restraint. When Dawn finally fell quiet, the Madame exhaled another cloud of smoke, her lips curling into something unreadable. "Very well," she murmured, her voice smooth as silk over steel. "I'll give you a chance. But don't disappoint me." Her gaze sharpened, the temperature of her words dropping. "Disappointment in my world is a very… expensive commodity."

Before Dawn could respond, danger prickled the air. The Professor's contact materialized from the shadows, smirking with insidious glee.

"Sorry, love," he drawled, his voice dripping with mock regret. "It's what I do. You're not the first, nor will you be the last."

The ambush was swift. Henchmen lunged from all sides, a swarm of muscle and malice. Dawn fought like hell, every strike calculated, every movement fluid and precise. She took down one, then another, but the odds were against her. A sharp prick at her neck—then darkness swallowed her.

As the dust settled, Sal emerged from the carnage, greed glistening in his beady eyes. He approached Madame Evangeline with a lecherous grin, nudging Dawn's unconscious form with his boot.

"Such a beauty, don't you think? Far superior to most. Perhaps you might increase the rate… or allow ol' Sal a taste before she's sold off?"

Silence stretched.

Evangeline turned, her gaze locking onto Sal with a thousand unspoken threats. Her expression was restrained fury, her lips curving into a ghost of a smile that held no warmth—only the promise of ruin.

The look alone was enough.

Sal paled, swallowing hard as understanding dawned. He scurried off like vermin, his bravado withering under her silent wrath.

Evangeline watched him go, exhaling a stream of smoke before turning back to the unconscious girl at her feet. "Such a waste… or perhaps, such potential," she mused softly, her voice barely audible beneath the pulse of the Inferno.

ABDUCTION AND AWAKENING

Darkness.

A crushing, suffocating void. Then, a slow, agonizing return to consciousness. Pain pulsed through Dawn's skull in relentless waves, each throb a cruel reminder that she was alive. Her body felt leaden, limbs unresponsive as though submerged in thick, unyielding tar. The cold, damp floor sent a sharp chill through her skin, rough stone pressing against her cheek. Rope bit into her wrists; her hands throbbed.

Panic seized her throat, coiling like a serpent. She swallowed hard, forcing it down. Where was she? What had happened?

Her vision wavered as shadows slowly took shape, revealing a small, claustrophobic cell. Rough-hewn walls loomed around her, slick with moisture and neglect. The only light came from a single, flickering torch on the far wall, its glow casting grotesque shadows that danced like specters. The air was thick—rancid with mildew, sweat, and something deeper that stank of despair and suffering.

She wasn't alone.

In the dim light, two figures huddled against the far wall, curled inward as though trying to disappear into the stone. Their eyes, hollow and vacant, stared through her rather than at her, filled with a fear that had long since stopped pleading for salvation. They were women— captives, just like her.

One was young, barely out of her teens, her body frail from malnourishment. Her dark eyes were wide with unspoken terror, darting between Dawn and the entrance as though expecting a monster to appear. Her name was Sarah, a runaway from the Outer World who had fled a broken home with dreams of escape, only to find herself ensnared in a nightmare far worse than what she'd left. Her tattered dress barely clung to her thin frame, the fabric soiled with grime and despair.

The other woman—Elena—was older, perhaps in her late thirties. Once, she might have been beautiful, a dancer moving effortlessly under a spotlight. Now, her skin was sallow, her lips pressed into a grim line of resignation. She had been promised a better life, lured with the illusion of opportunity, only to be betrayed and dragged into this abyss. Her eyes no longer held fear, only the dull acceptance of someone who had already lost hope.

"Don't scream," a voice rasped from the shadows.

Dawn's heart slammed against her ribs as she turned toward the source. Elena's voice was barely more than a breath, a whisper coated in dread. "He'll come back sooner, and he'll take one of us. The last girl didn't listen. She screamed... and she hasn't come back. I think you're her replacement."

Dawn's pulse quickened, nausea curling in her stomach. She strained to push herself upright, the damp stone chilling her through torn clothing.

"Where are we? What's going on?" Her voice was hoarse, cracking with fear. "What do you mean, 'replacement'?"

Elena's gaze flickered toward the door as if expecting it to burst open. "I don't know," she admitted, her voice trembling. "I was on my way to a show. Next thing I knew, I woke up here. There were others... two more girls. They were taken a few days ago." She hesitated, her breath shaky. "I don't think they're coming back."

A leaden weight settled in Dawn's gut. She knew exactly what kind of "replacement" they meant.

"How long have you been here?" she asked, barely above a whisper.

Elena exhaled slowly. "A week, maybe."

Dawn licked dry lips. "What's your name?"

The older woman opened her mouth—but her entire body stiffened. Terror swept across her face. She pressed a trembling finger to her lips.

Footsteps.

Heavy. Measured. A shadow stretched across the entrance, growing larger as something approached. Then a hulking figure filled the doorway, broad silhouette outlined against the dim torchlight. He loomed there, unmoving, his presence thick and suffocating.

The air turned ice-cold.

Dawn's breath caught as he took a slow step forward. He was monstrous—filthy and unkempt, clothes tattered and stained. The stench of sweat and decay clung to him like a second skin. His face was obscured by a crude mask, but she could see his eyes gleaming beneath it, hungry and void of humanity.

Lionel Lawson.

The name clawed its way into her mind, unraveling the horrifying truth. He was the hidden son of Ryne Lawson, the secret she had helped conceal. Once sheltered, once protected—but no longer. Exiled to the Outer World, Lionel had been consumed by bitterness, twisted into a creature of pure depravity. He was no longer a man. He was a tool—an instrument of Madame Evangeline's will, a predator shaped by the nightmares of the damned.

His massive hand shot forward, seizing Elena by the arm.

She screamed.

A raw, piercing cry of desperation shattered the stale air.

Sarah gasped, curling into herself as sobs wracked her frail body. Dawn felt her own heart hammering, the sound deafening in her ears. Every muscle in her body tensed as she watched Elena struggle, nails raking against his grip, terror spilling out in strangled pleas. There was no mercy in Lionel's eyes. He yanked her forward, her feet dragging across the floor.

No.

Dawn's breath came in ragged bursts, her mind racing. She couldn't let this happen.

Training and instinct took over.

She exploded into motion.

Her knee slammed into his spine, the impact reverberating through her hip. He was solid, almost unyielding.

He turned, surprisingly quick, and caught her by the throat.

Shit.

Stone cracked against her back as he thrust her into the wall, pain flaring down her limbs. No time for pain. No time for air.

She twisted, driving her knee up repeatedly—hard—into his stomach, then groin. The air left him in a sharp grunt, his grip loosening just enough.

Dawn didn't hesitate.

A sharp elbow to his jaw. A kick to his knee.

Weak points. Always go for the weak points.

He staggered, but it wasn't enough.

So she made it enough.

Her fingers closed around a loose stone on the floor, jagged and solid—a weapon granted by chance. With all the strength she could muster, she drove it into his temple. A roar of agony ripped from him as he reeled back, clutching his head. Dawn pressed her advantage, striking again and again with her bound hands, targeting pressure points, exploiting every weakness she could find. Each blow carried every ounce of rage, fear, and determination she had left.

With one final, desperate heave, she sent him crashing to the ground. His body hit the floor with a sickening thud, his mask slipping free.

What lay beneath chilled Dawn to the bone.

The features that stared back were twisted, scarred—and unsettlingly childlike. A face that should have been innocent but was contorted by unchecked darkness, a man caught between boyhood and the perversion he'd been allowed to fester.

Dawn swallowed the revulsion rising in her throat and turned to the others, breathing hard.

"We have to get out of here," she said, urgency slicing through her voice. "Now."

Elena shook her head violently, her eyes wild. "There's nowhere to go! This is the Outer World! It's all the same—hell!"

Dawn refused to accept that.

"We're not staying here," she said, steel in her tone. "We're getting out. Are you with me?"

A pause. Fear battled with hope. Then, slowly, one by one, they nodded.

Working together, they fumbled with Dawn's restraints, loosening them enough for her to wriggle free. Once her hands were loose, she wasted no time unbinding the others, her movements swift and precise.

"Stay close," Dawn ordered, leading them toward the exit. "And be ready for anything."

Sarah clung to her arm, trembling. "I'm scared. What's out there?"

Dawn glanced at the looming darkness beyond, at the unknown horrors that surely awaited. Her voice, however, remained steady.

"Worse than this, probably," she admitted. "But we'll face it together."

And with that, they stepped forward into whatever awaited them beyond the prison of their pasts.

25 DYSTOPIAN ESCAPE

The tunnels reeked of rot and mildew. The walls dripped. Somewhere in the distance, someone moaned—weak, broken.

Their only source of light was a makeshift torch, a rag doused in oil scavenged from their captor, now flickering weakly in Dawn's trembling grip. Shadows danced wildly across the walls, morphing into grotesque shapes that seemed to breathe with a life of their own.

Dawn tightened her hold on the torch. They had to keep moving.

Every shadow was a potential threat, every corner a place for something to lurk. Elena and Sarah clung to her heels, their fear tangible, their breaths shallow and rapid.

As they pressed deeper into the underground abyss, they encountered others—prisoners like them, though some had long since surrendered to despair. Hollow-eyed and emaciated, they shuffled through the darkness with lifeless gazes, existing more as specters than survivors. Others had lost not just hope but sanity, their minds broken by captivity, reduced to snarling, feral husks of what they once were.

Their wild, darting eyes carried no recognition, only the raw hunger of those starved for both food and freedom.

A man stumbled toward them, his face a map of scars and suffering, his trembling hand reaching for salvation. "Help me… please… HELP ME…" His voice cracked with desperation.

Sarah hesitated, her heart twisting, guilt weighing on every breath. She turned away, squeezing her eyes shut. "I'm sorry, I can't."

Elena grabbed her arm, pulling her along. "Don't look. There's nothing we can do."

Each step felt like an eternity, but at last, they found an exit—a narrow passage slanting upward, a sliver of dim light spilling through cracks above. The sight of it should have been a relief, but instead it only deepened the unease in Dawn's gut. She halted at the threshold, her pulse hammering in her ears.

"I don't like this," she murmured. "It's too quiet."

Sarah shivered. "What if it's a trap?"

Dawn tightened her grip on the torch. "Then we'll deal with it. Get ready."

Taking a deep breath, she stepped forward, the others close behind.

The passage opened into a crumbling alleyway, a gaping wound in the heart of what was once civilization. The air was thick with toxic haze, each breath burning their throats, the distant glow of fires casting an eerie orange hue over the cityscape.

As the sun began to set, urgency spread between them.

"We have to find shelter, some place safe to hide," Sarah urged, tugging at Dawn's arm.

"Safe? There's no such thing here. You'd better grow up, kid," Elena snapped.

"Then we'll make it safe. Stay close, and do what I say." Dawn grabbed Sarah's hand and squeezed it, a brief, warm pressure.

They ventured into the heart of the Outer World, moving cautiously through the ruined streets. Dawn kept her hand near the makeshift knife she'd fashioned from broken glass, scanning every doorway and alleyway for threats. Scavengers prowled the ruins, sunken faces and bony fingers scratching through rubble for anything of value.

A grizzled scavenger stepped into their path, his eyes narrowed. "What do you want?" he growled, murmurs rippling through the group behind him as hands tightened on improvised weapons.

"We're just passing through. We mean no harm," Dawn said. Her tone was unassuming, but her stance made the message clear: she was not to be tested.

"Can we rest here for a sec?" Elena asked.

"You don't belong here. Go back where you came from." His cataract-clouded eyes told them to get lost.

"We have nowhere else to go," Sarah said, her eyes shining.

"You can go to hell for all I care!" he shouted.

At his signal, the scavengers surged forward with bad intentions.

"Run," Dawn snapped.

Elena and Sarah bolted without hesitation.

Predatory gangs ruled these streets, moving with the feral confidence of wolves. Dawn knew better than to stand and trade blows; survival here meant choosing when not to fight. They needed cover, a plan, and time to breathe—but first, they had to live long enough to find it.

They couldn't stay. They needed a plan, a place to hide, a moment to think. But survival came first. Dawn assessed the chaos, remembering her orders: continue the quest through a world full of violent drug addicts, sadistic pimps, mutant henchmen, warring gangs, and any number of despicable refuse ejected from Secure City. Maintain her cover. Suppress potentially lethal altercations. And somehow, eventually, find the missing student.

As they ventured deeper into the desolate expanse, a chill crept up Dawn's spine. Someone was watching—and it wasn't Matthew's drone. She felt it in the weight of the air, in the prickling unease settling into her bones. This was no simple escape.

She was a pawn in a much larger game, and the stakes were higher than she'd ever imagined.

Every step was a gamble; every choice could mean life or death. She'd have to find safety for Elena and Sarah and somehow connect them to Matthew for safe passage. The challenge seemed daunting, but the ultimate objective left her no alternative:

Return to the Inferno. Find Madame Evangeline. Convince her it was in her best interest to disclose the student's location.

And by convince, she meant unleashing mayhem—culminating in excruciating amounts of pain and destruction.

26 RAYNE LAWSON'S SHADOW

The air of the Outer World was thick with an acrid blend of decay and despair, a cruel contrast to the clinical sterility of the Secure Cities. Dawn moved with purpose, her steps calculated, her senses finely attuned to the ever-present danger in the shadows. The ruins of what had once been a thriving metropolis loomed around her—skeletal buildings standing defiantly against time, broken windows like hollow eyes staring into an abyss. Here, lawlessness reigned, and whispers of the dead and forgotten clung to the walls like a malignant echo.

She couldn't shake the feeling that Ryne Lawson's presence lingered in the undercurrents of this decayed world. A name that carried the weight of a thundercloud.

Ryne Lawson—a widow veiled in opulence and influence, her wealth an empire built on generations of shadowed dealings. To the world, she was a philanthropist, a woman of status who grieved her husband's loss with grace, channeling her resources into charity. But beneath the polished façade, she was the puppeteer of a dark empire, her fingers entwined in the criminal underbelly that dictated the unspoken rules of power.

A name spoken only in hushed voices had led Dawn here, deeper into the tangled web of the Hundred Project—a mystery whose roots reached into the foundations of the Secure Cities and the desolation beyond their walls. Her investigation into the abductions had traced a trail of blood and vanished souls to one undeniable link:

Ryne Lawson.

And with that name came another, even more dangerous:

Lionel Lawson.

"Lionel?" Sal rasped, his voice raw from years of inhaling the Outer World's poisoned air. His weathered fingers twitched nervously as he glanced over his shoulder, as if the name alone could summon wrath. "That's a name you don't breathe around here, doll. Ryne Lawson's got ears everywhere, and she don't take kindly to folks askin' 'bout her boy."

The rumors painted a grotesque picture—a man of towering strength and shattered sanity, his mind a labyrinth of twisted urges left unchecked by a mother whose influence silenced justice. Lionel Lawson was no ordinary threat; he was a creature born of indulgence and impunity, his darkest desires shielded by his mother's wealth. Ryne had concealed his crimes, twisted the law into her own web of deception, until his monstrous urges grew beyond even her reach.

That was when Charles Partlow—the former Agency man whose life Dawn had ended—uncovered the truth.

Partlow had not sought justice; he had sought leverage. A government agent who had once stood on the side of order, he had instead become an accomplice, a partner in Ryne's wicked empire. He whispered his findings not to authorities, but to Ryne herself, twisting his knowledge into a means of control. Their relationship spiraled into something darker—a perverse entanglement of power, control, and shared corruption.

Before his death, Partlow had bared his sins to Dawn, his voice a rasp of confession and regret.

"She helped me discover my true passion," he had murmured, his eyes alight with something far beyond repentance. "I loved her for it… Everything was perfect for years. She lived the perfect life… I was the highly decorated government agent… nobody even suspected we knew each other…"

Yet even Ryne's wealth and reach had limits. Lionel, the beast she had shielded for so long, grew too wild and unpredictable. His strength grew. His crimes escalated beyond quiet whispers and secret bribes.

Partlow had suggested the unthinkable: exile.

The Outer World—lawless and ungoverned—would become Lionel's new domain, a place where his unchecked darkness could roam free, a creature unleashed upon a forsaken world. Desperate to preserve her own power, Ryne agreed. But in doing so, she did not save her son.

She cast him into the arms of something far worse.

In the wasteland, Lionel found a new master: Madame Evangeline. A name spoken with equal parts reverence and fear, she ruled the depraved, a queen of the forsaken. Under her influence, Lionel became more than a man—he became a force, a legend whispered in terror.

And now, with the reemergence of abductions in Secure City 24, Dawn could feel the tendrils of Ryne Lawson's influence reaching forth once more.

Was Ryne orchestrating these horrors from the safety of her ivory tower, her son the monster she unleashed upon the world? Or was something even more insidious at play—a scheme that reached beyond cruelty, entwining itself with the very fabric of the Secure Cities and the silent war waged beneath their polished surface?

Dawn's mission had always been dangerous, but now it had become something else—a descent into the past, into the very heart of darkness itself. The truth lay buried in Ryne Lawson's carefully guarded secrets, and Dawn would stop at nothing to unearth it.

Because in the shadows, where power played its silent games, the greatest monsters were not those born of the Outer World's chaos, but those who had built the walls to keep it at bay.

And Ryne Lawson was the key—not just to the abductions, but to the Hundred Project and the threads that bound them all.

EPILOGUE

This assignment was off the books, a plan devised in the afterglow. Matthew couldn't keep his eyes off Dawn; it was finally over. They could breathe freely, be themselves together—or so he assumed—but he couldn't shake the uneasiness he sensed in her.

"I know you like I know myself; your poker face doesn't work with me." He shifted back on top of her, slowly lowering himself, kissing and tasting the salt of her sweat-covered skin. "Better spill it if you don't want me to stop." He dipped lower, nibbling the skin around her toned abs.

She quivered as he softly bit. "I'll tell you once you've finished."

"You promise?"

She said nothing, but he knew she was a woman of her word with him. Her only response was the soft caress of his ears as her hands guided him to his destination.

Afterward, she finally spoke—the ongoing conflict within her, the uncertainty, the fragmented vision of who she thought she was and what she might be. The continuous nightmares. The battle inside. Everything except her deepest secret.

Like an addict in withdrawal, she fought it, convincing herself— mind over matter—that she was in control, but she knew it was a lie. The desires burned like an inferno. And even though she loved Matthew, their shared passion felt like a temporary balm on a gaping wound, a fleeting moment of peace in a world of unending war. She needed answers, a definitive truth to either shatter or solidify her existence.

Matthew stirred beside her, sensing the turmoil beneath her calm façade. "What's really going on?" he asked softly.

She hesitated, the weight of her secrets pressing down. "It's… the Professor," she admitted at last, the name a bitter taste on her tongue. "I need to know."

Matthew's expression hardened; something sank in his gut. But if their love was ever going to breathe in daylight, there had to be closure.

The Professor's home: an encrypted file hidden in a wall safe in the study.

Matthew had mentioned it more than once. The mission: violate his trust and manipulate him as he had so often manipulated them. Accessing those files was the objective.

It wouldn't be easy, but it was far from the most dangerous work they'd done, and they approached it with the same focus and seriousness as any other op.

Disconnect the alarm. Redirect camera feeds. Neutralize the security detail. Follow protocol. Acquire the package without a hitch.

Under the cloak of a starless night, they infiltrated the Professor's opulent residence. The air hung heavy with the smell of old money and unspoken sins.

Dawn moved with practiced grace, senses honed to a razor's edge. Matthew, a ghost in his childhood home, guided her through the labyrinthine corridors, his face a mask of grim determination.

"He always kept the security system state-of-the-art," Matthew murmured, his fingers dancing over a keypad. "But I know his patterns. He's predictable in his own twisted way."

With the alarm disarmed, they slipped into the study—the heart of the Professor's empire of knowledge and manipulation. Bookshelves stretched toward the high ceiling, leather-bound spines whispering secrets in the dim light. The air was thick with aged paper and power.

"The safe is behind that portrait," Matthew said, pointing to a life-sized painting of Evelyn. "He always kept it close, like a shrine."

Dawn approached the portrait, tracing the familiar features of the woman whose genetic echo resonated within her. A wave of conflicting emotion washed over her—pity, resentment, and a strange sense of connection to this woman she had never known.

She looked around, struck by a sad, painful epiphany. Despite all her encounters with the Professor, she had never been beyond the public spaces of his home—not even his bedroom. Their entanglements were inappropriate and far from romantic. She gazed at the painting of the woman he loved, the woman she'd been created to resemble, and understood: she wasn't his lover.

She was his outlet.

Matthew worked swiftly. With a click, the portrait swung aside, revealing the steel door of the safe. His fingers flew over the tumblers, the combination a ghost from his past.

"Got it," he breathed, pulling open the heavy door.

Inside, nestled among stacks of currency and classified documents, was a single encrypted drive.

As they decrypted the file, a cascade of images and text flooded the screen, revealing the horrifying scope of Project Doppelganger. Cloning. Resurrection. Genetic manipulation. The Professor had delved into forbidden depths in his desperate attempt to cheat death and control destiny.

But the most chilling revelation was the truth about Matthew.

The file detailed that after Evelyn's death in a car crash, her son—Matthew—had been stillborn. The Professor, consumed by grief and obsession, secretly harvested genetic material from both Evelyn and the infant.

Matthew stood frozen, his face ashen. "Stillborn… So… what am I?" he choked, his voice barely audible. "Just another one of his experiments?"

Dawn reached out, gripping his hand tightly. "No, Matthew," she said fiercely. "You're not. You're you. You made your own choices, forged your own path. He doesn't own you."

But even as she spoke, unease settled over her. The files hinted at something more—a hidden layer to the Professor's design that remained shrouded in mystery.

By unlocking the file, Dawn and Matthew had unknowingly opened Pandora's box. They'd found the answers they sought—but they had also unleashed a new tide of questions, a dark current that threatened to engulf them both.

The war was far from over.

It had only just begun.

ABOUT THE AUTHOR

Andre LaVelle is a multi-hyphenate autodidact polymath whose work lives at the intersection of visual art, performance, and storytelling. A Chicago native, he got his start at Simeon Vocational High School, majoring in Commercial Art under William Myles, the teacher who pushed him past comic books and cartoons into a broader creative world.

Building on that spark, LaVelle studied photography at Columbia College Chicago, drawing inspiration from icons like Gordon Parks, Herb Ritts, Richard Avedon, and Victor Skrebneski. His eye for image and story led him into art direction, music videos, and film, and ultimately to founding LVI Studios in Los Angeles, where his bold visuals and the acclaimed Phantasy calendar series—and its companion documentary—earned national and international attention.

Onstage, LaVelle sharpened his comedic voice in clubs across Chicago before taking his talents to Hollywood, where he soaked up every angle of moviemaking as a producer, writer, actor, and director. During the pandemic, he poured that experience onto the page, writing seventeen scripts—several of which he transformed into novels, including *Dawn Knight*.

Relentlessly curious and impossible to box in, Andre LaVelle continues to create on his own terms, blending image, humor, and heart into stories that feel as lived-in as they are larger than life.